She Who Turns the Vampire

K. MALADY

Copyright © 2025 by K. Malady

All rights reserved.

No portion of this book may be reproduced in any form without written permission from the publisher or author, except as permitted by U.S. copyright law.

This novel's story and characters are fictitious. Names, characters, business, places, events, and incidents are the products of the author's imagination or used in a fictitious manner. Any resemblance to actual persons, living or dead (or mythological), or actual events is purely coincidental.

Cover by Getcovers

Also By

THE ASCEND TRIALS
YA fantasy romance adventure

THE HARMONY CHRONICLES
NA paranormal romance/contemporary fantasy

THREADS OF FATE
NA/Adult romantic fantasy retellings

KNEELING KINGDOMS
Adult interconnected standalone romantasy

OICHE

Atharra

Laidir

Fuil

Heroi

Bec

Oracle

Giobas

The Aboveground

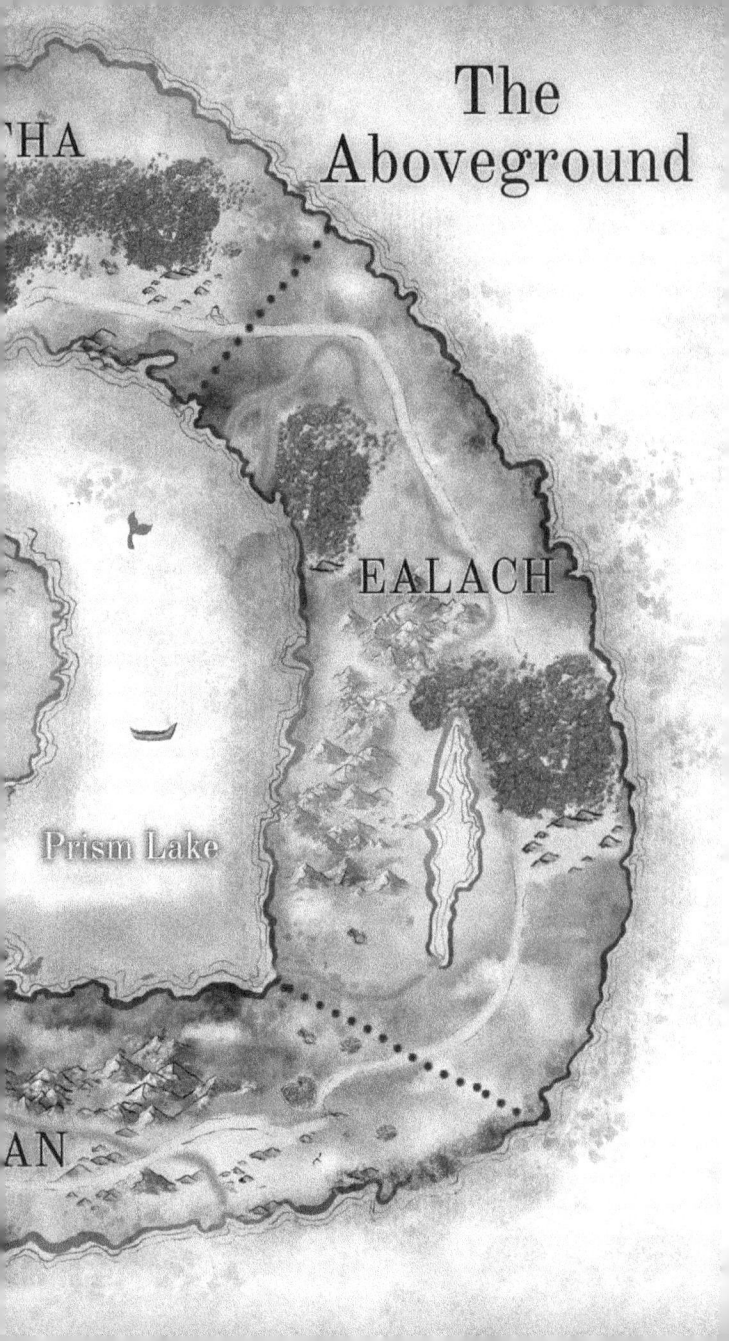

'HA

EALACH

Prism Lake

AN

Avalaruin

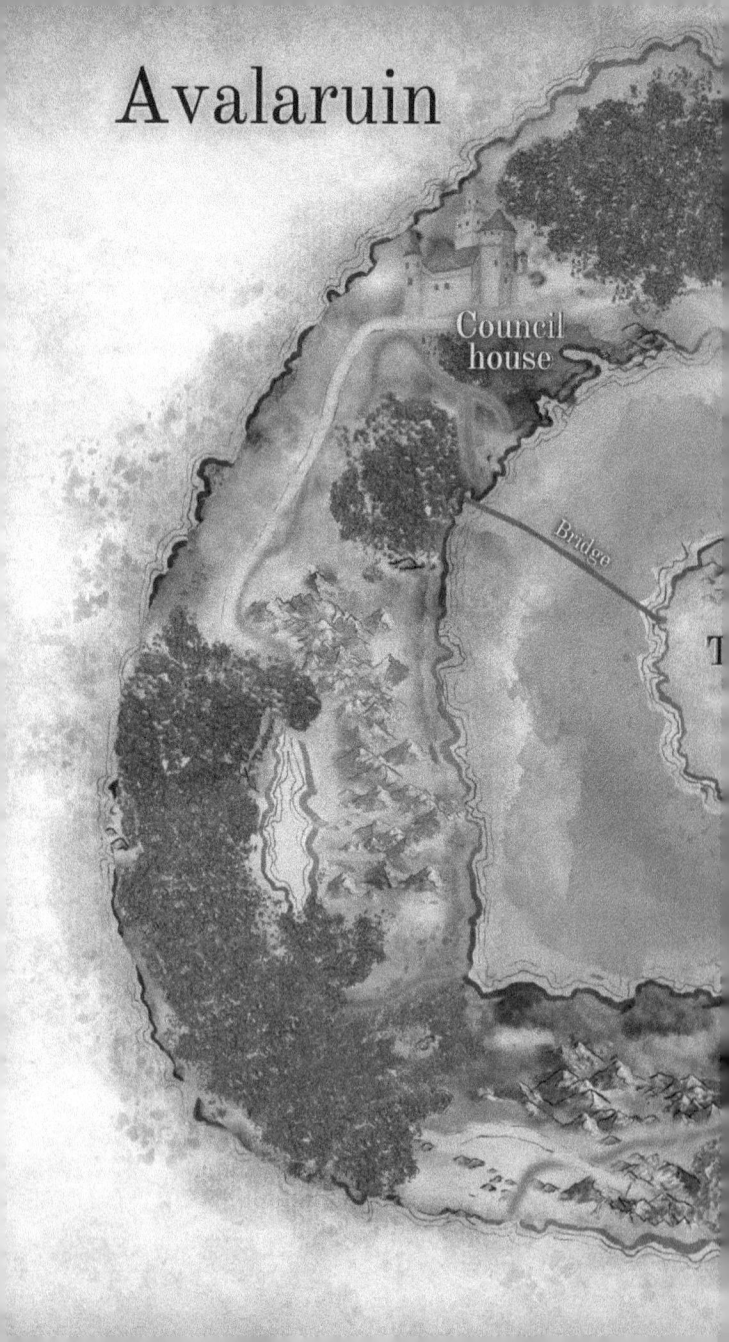

Council house

Bridge

Castle

Bridge

Unseen Lake

Emma's Diary Entry

5th day of the Flower Moon, 1909

Dear Diary,

I was wrong. I had *every* intention of putting my foot down with Clara and refusing to attend Demara's party. Yet, somehow, she swayed me.

I told her repeatedly, in a tone better suited to my youngest cousins than a thirty-year-old vampire princess, that I *wasn't* going. Of course, vampire princesses are allowed their petulant moments. It's the thirty-year-old part that makes it slightly embarrassing in hindsight.

The sunlight poured through the stained glass windows of my room, creating colorful patterns across the floor, as if mocking my irritation. I wanted to be anywhere but there—out in the world, having fun, not stuck playing nice with dignitaries.

"Your presence is not negotiable," Clara declared, her face pinched and unimpressed, as usual. You'd think she'd be used to my antics by now—she's been managing them since I was a child. Already dressed for the occasion in her red gown, her silver hair braided tightly into a crown, she looked every inch the enforcer of my duties.

"You are heir to the throne," she reminded me, as if I could ever forget. "You must attend Demara's ball and show respect to the leader of the Turned."

I spun around on my heel, the lace at my cuffs fluttering, a bit dramatically, if I'm honest. I was wearing that Avalaruin blouse I bought last year. You remember the one, made of spun spidersilk by one of those odd lesser fae the prince keeps around.

"I'd rather make nice with a stake," I muttered, flopping onto the chaise lounge with as much flair as possible.

SHE WHO TURNS THE VAMPIRE

The leader—*Wilson*? *Willy*?—had been in power over the Turned vampires long before I was born. Everything I've heard about him paints him as a stick-in-the-mud, obsessed with rules and far too proud of being one of the first Turned vampires.

As I traced idle patterns on the armrest, I asked, "Can't Demara handle it? She lives for this sort of thing—diplomacy, negotiations, pretending she doesn't despise everyone in the room. Besides, rumor has it she even convinced the fae prince to show up."

"Emma," Clara sighed, the sound heavy and authoritative, as though calling me to some solemn duty. "As second in line for the throne, your attendance sends a message of unity to the Turned. Whether or not you enjoy it, these alliances are vital to our future."

"This is just a ball for Demara's suitors, not anything *important*." I rolled my eyes, though I felt a slight flutter in my chest—the persistent anxiety of knowing that if anything happened to Demara, I'd be the one forced to step up. Honestly, she needs to have an heir, so I can avoid ever being put in that position. "Couldn't we reschedule?"

"The two hundredth anniversary of the birth of the Turned conclave is approaching," Clara explained. "It's vital to commemorate our connection with the Turned and honor our treaty with the humans."

"Two hundred years feels like a long weekend to us," I said with a dismissive wave of my hand, the light glinting off the jewels on my wrist. "We've been allies since... well, forever."

"Allies for *under* two hundred years, Emma," Clara corrected, her tone patient but firm. She has centuries on me, after all, and likely sees me as something of a child. "This event memorializes their coming into power, a step that led to the treaty. And I was alive then, so let me remind you—those early years were filled with violence and chaos before we finally achieved peace."

I sighed, exaggeratedly, of course. "It sounds dreadful. Thank goodness it's ancient history.."

"History you should care about," she countered, arms crossed in that way that makes me want to do the exact opposite of whatever she suggests. "Especially with Demara's suitors circling. You need to show respect for the alliances we've built while Demara forges new ones."

"I respect alliances," I said. "I survived lunch with Aunt Petunia last week, didn't I? If that doesn't demonstrate patience and respect, I don't know what does."

Clara narrowed her eyes at me. "The relationships between us—the Aislean, the Turned, the humans, and even the fae—are delicate. Ignorance isn't bliss; it's dangerous."

And then she did it, Diary. Her next argument convinced me to change my mind.

"If you don't attend," she said, with the weight of centuries behind her words, "I will schedule meeting after meeting with dignitaries until you don't have a free moment for the next century."

I blanched at the thought. Imagining my days filled with endless formalities and conversations with dull dignitaries… I'd likely die. "Fine, fine," I relented. "I'll go to the ridiculous ball. But only for ten minutes."

"Thirty," Clara countered. "And I won't make you dance with anyone."

So, now I'm dressed in that lovely blue gown from last Samhain—the one that matches my eyes and has a pocket perfectly sized for this diary, you remember.

Clara is at the door, waiting. I'm starting the clock the moment I step out. Let's see if I can turn this tedious night into something *slightly* more adventurous.

Note from Clara

Emma, before you meet with the Turned leader, it would benefit you to review the notes from my prior lectures on the subject. I've compiled your personal notes, but am unsurprised to see that they are lacking.

Do try harder next time,
Clara

Class Notes

Unread since first written by Emma at age fifteen.

THE HISTORY OF THE Aislean and the Turned

For centuries, there were only the Aislean—vampires born that way, distinguished by our ability to walk in the daylight and, of course, live for an awfully long time. We thrived on blood (still do, naturally), but can go without. We were given this land by the Fae, snuggled between the mages and non-magical humans in the Aboveground.

Then came the problem of those vampires who didn't care much for propriety and dined on whomever they pleased—much to the irritation of humans, who, it turns out, weren't too keen on being prey.

~~(To be fair, it isn't as though we can drink a human's blood without killing them. It comes with the immortality bit. We drink, even a teaspoon, humans die. So maybe those bad vampires were simply *really* thirsty?)~~

Enter the Fae: They, in their benevolence (or perhaps just frustration at the mess), decided to intervene. The High King of the Fae (Bearach, super old, has a kid my age, super cute) demanded that the Aislean find a way to coexist with humans without depleting them entirely—or else we'd be facing his wrath, which, by all accounts, would have been quite unpleasant. I happen to like my castle at Fuil. The fae were about to attack the vampires—all of us, good and bad—and the bad ones were frothing at the mouth for it.

But then a mage (whose name no one bothered to remember, so were they really all that important?) appeared. They came up with a solution: a potion that allowed humans to be turned into vampires rather than simply becoming a meal. A human drinks a potion and a vampire feeds, and so is born a Turned. Vampires get to drink, humans get to live, kind of. These new vampires created their own little hierarchy, though they'll never be quite the same as the Aislean. (They do try, though.)

The Turned: something something... Clara was talking too fast! One was made, and then another, and then someone of Aislean royalty made one and created a royal branch, I suppose. The Turned got a pocket of our realm for themselves, based in Atharra.

The Treaty: Once the potion was approved and Bearach dealt with those bad vampires, peace came. And to prevent further... disagreements between humans and vampires, the fae established a treaty. Vampires—both Aislean and Turned—are bound by magic to avoid feeding on any human who doesn't want to be Turned. In those cases, we must find other sources of blood (cow's blood, for instance, though it's a far cry from the real thing). If a vampire does break this rule and takes a human's life anyway, well... it's not good. Exile, imprisonment, or worse. All depends on how furious the fae are, and they do tend to find out. One must be cautious.

The Future: To be determined. Apparently the Turned still have some complaints? (Likely that we're a reminder of what they can't do: pass along the curse and live a full life, rather than the half-life of a vampire who cannot walk in the sun). Fingers crossed Demara has an heir before I accidentally inherit the throne. I'd rather she deal with it.

Emma's Diary Entry

5th day of the Flower Moon, that evening

Diary,

A quick update while I wait for Lysandra's return—I've found a way to make this dreadful evening bearable!

Surprisingly, when I arrived at the ball, the grandeur of it all briefly distracted me from my boredom. The castle's ancient ballroom, usually so dreary, had been transformed into a starlit dreamscape. The ceiling shimmered with charmed constellations, courtesy of one of our mage party-planners. Gossamer curtains billowed softly in the breeze, scented with night-blooming flowers from the garden.

The aristocracy was draped in hues of midnight blue, blood red, and moon silver, their finery echoing the haunting melody played by the string quartet. Crystal chandeliers hung like frozen raindrops, but it was the soft glow of the new electric lights that truly enchanted the space. I'd had them installed recently—a human invention I find fascinating—and they brought brightness and clarity to the room in a way candlelight never could.

"Remember, Emma," Clara had reminded me as I descended the staircase, "tonight is more than a celebration. Demara will announce her suitors—a pivotal moment for our lineage. You have a role to play."

Honestly, our society's obsession with parading suitors like prized stallions is embarrassing. All for the sake of alliances and noble bloodlines. It's twisted—bonds forged not by passion but by political strategy. But I digress.

Although first I must record my own romantic misstep. After treading through the sea of swaying bodies, I found Phaeron, his white-blond hair a striking contrast against the dark uniforms of the castle guard. He was standing, statuesque and ever vigilant, near the grand archway that framed the ballroom's entrance. His chiseled jaw was set with duty, but those black eyes held a softness that made me bold enough to approach.

"Phaeron," I purred, gliding up to him like a cat who'd caught sight of an enticing mouse. Although Phaeron is no mouse—he's more like a lion I long to tame. "Care to abandon your post for a dance?"

I tilted my head back just enough for my golden curls to cascade down my back in what I've been told was an irresistible display. But Phaeron didn't waver.

"Princess Emma," he replied, his voice low and smooth, cutting through the music and chatter. "I'm afraid my duties tonight extend beyond the dance floor."

He nodded towards two figures at the edge of the room—the fae envoys. They were ethereal, their golden skin glowing under the chandeliers, and the fae prince outshone everyone with his otherworldly radiance. His companion—a woman who looked like a voluptuous goddess—was stunning in her resplendent, shimmering gown.

I sighed, but couldn't resist a retort. "And here I thought the highlight of the evening would be dancing with you, not watching you play chaperone."

"Your sister's commands were quite explicit," Phaeron said with a trace of amusement. "I must ensure that all diplomatic relations remain... cordial."

I wish I could say I saw a flicker of regret in his expression, but honestly, Diary—I don't think it was for me. More likely, he was simply intrigued by the fae woman. I sighed again, turning away with a *partially* feigned pout. "Of course. The fate of nations rests on your broad shoulders. Better yours than mine."

Leaving him to his duties, I wove my way through the clusters of nobles and dignitaries, their perfumes mingling into a dizzying cloud. Finally, I found Lysandra, her raven-black hair and sharp eyes a welcome sight as she lounged against a pillar.

"Can you believe it?" I huffed, collapsing beside her. "Phaeron is stuck babysitting the fae. As if I needed another reason to despise these insufferable pageants."

"Ah, Emma," Lysandra teased, a glint in her eyes as she smoothed down her sapphire gown. "You always did have a taste for the unattainable."

"Unattainable and maddening," I muttered, watching Phaeron as he guided the fae prince and his companion into a dance. I shook my head. "And to think Clara threatened me with endless meetings if I didn't attend tonight. As if I don't have better things to do than sit in on dreary conferences."

"Like plotting ways to lure tall, stoic guardsmen from their posts?" Lysandra winked, clearly enjoying herself.

"Obviously," I said. "But enough talk. I suppose I need to find William, Willis, Wallis, whoever the Turned leader is."

"Or," Lysandra whispered, her hand slipping into mine—a touch that promised escape, "we take a little drive."

I looked at her, wide-eyed. "You've got a..."

She smirked, leaning closer. "Mother bought me an auto."

An *auto*! We're risking everything, I know—being in a wooden contraption is practically flirting with death for a vampire. But isn't life about taking risks? As we speak, Lysandra is gathering the others. I'm sitting just outside the castle gates, scribbling this by the light of one of my marvelous electric lamps. I'll check in later—perhaps after a daring adventure behind the wheel.

MALLORY'S MECHANIZED MARVELS PRESENTS

THE 1906 AUTOMOBILE

A human invention so clever, even mages are jealous!

BEHOLD THE FUTURE!

Speed Without Spells: Outruns werewolves, outshines broomsticks!

Powered by Petrol: No magic, just brilliant human engineering!

Stylish & Spacious: Seats four (or a dozen pixies)!

ONLY 12,000 COINS!

Warning: Automobile not guaranteed to function around ley lines, or in areas saturated with chaos magic. Please consult your local mage or mechanic for maintenance.

Emma's Diary Entry

Still the 5th day of the Flower Moon, that evening

Dear Diary,

First things first: the automobile. Our chariot of freedom, a gleaming black beauty with an engine that purred like a contented cat. It's a marvel of human ingenuity, a bold statement of progress. I wanted to linger, trace my fingers over its smooth frame, but time wasn't on our side. And now, we might never get that chance again.

But I'm getting ahead of myself.

Once we made it outside, I quickly ushered everyone into the seats, the plush velvet cushions welcoming us warmly.

Let me start from the beginning. We were all crammed into the auto, sinking into the plush velvet seats, Cerdan complimenting how I looked behind the wheel. I imagine we were quite the sight, barreling down the winding cobblestone path away from Fuil and into the dense forest. Laughter bubbled from us as we sped through the night, the wind tousling my hair, the streetlamps turning into streaks of light as the world blurred around us. It was exhilarating, wild, as though we had left all our worries in the distant castle.

We quickly left the forest behind us, bursting through the trees into the outlying mage settlement of Bec. It's a small community inhabited by a single coven, with a lovely view of the secondary selkie settlement on Prism Lake. The perfect place to watch the colors dance and indulge in some magical hallucinogens.

The mages' homes emerged from the darkness, an eccentric collection of hovels and shacks that look like they grew organically from the earth itself. We slowed to a stop, the automobile's headlamps casting an eerie glow on the crooked signs and dangling herbs that ornament the cottages.

We wound our way through narrow alleys lined with blooming nightshade and twisted brambles, each step stirring up whispers from hidden corners. Finally, we found our destination: a modest cottage adorned with glowing sigils and dried flowers hanging above the doorway. Moss clung to its wooden panels, giving it a sense of being slowly consumed by nature, and the thatched roof sagged under the weight of centuries.

The door creaked open to reveal an elderly mage with wise eyes that seemed to pierce through our very souls. She ushered us inside her hut where the room was bathed with a warm glow from burning candles that flickered like captive stars. The air was charged with old magic and a hint of something wild and untamed. Shelves lined with jars of shimmering powders and twisted roots loomed over us.

Her voice wavered with age as she asked what we sought, and I cheekily asked for something "transformative."

Her knowing smile gave away that she saw through our request. We weren't seeking enlightenment—we just wanted to get lost in the haze of a magical escape. Soon, she disappeared into the shadows of the room, rummaging through jars and vials. The silence stretched between us, broken only by the crackling of the fire in the hearth.

After what felt like forever, she handed me a vial filled with swirling, shifting colors. The scent was intoxicating, promising a dreamy escape. The contents undulated inside the glass, a mesmerizing kaleidoscope of colors and promise.

"This will take you where you need to go," she said, placing the vial in my outstretched hand.

Her touch was surprisingly gentle, but her grip tightened when I tried to pull away. "You've got places to be yourself, little lady."

The hairs on the back of my neck stood at attention, but I laughed it off. "I'm always on the move," I said glibly.

We bid the mage farewell and stepped out into the cool night air, quickly ingesting our prize. The potion tasted like liquid fire as it slid down our throats. Reality blurred around the edges as we made our way to the lake.

Lysandra leaned against me, her warmth seeping into my side as we sat on the rocky shore, Cerdan kneeling on the other side, and Alina curled around our feet. The moon painted a silvery path across the water, and the selkies danced in the light, their movements a poetry amplified by the magic coursing through us. Hours passed in a blissful haze, the world softening around us until, too soon, the effects began to fade.

"That was too fast," Cerdan complained, stretching and dislodging Alina from her comfortable position as the last of the magic dissipated.

"Are we sure it was a good batch?" Alina rubbed her hip where she fell into the sand.

"Yes," I murmured as the last traces of the potion's effects fade away. "We're just building up a tolerance."

Lysandra laughed and helped me up. "Looks like we'll have to find another vice."

"What's left?" I teased. "Let's drive back. Maybe nobody will notice we're gone."

We began our return, but halfway through the forest, our escapade came to an abrupt halt: the engine sputtered and died with a final wheeze, its mechanical death rattle echoing like a funeral dirge. I twisted the key again and again in desperation, but the car remained stubbornly silent.

Alina tried to cheer us up. "Maybe it's just resting? It carried us quite spiritedly through our escapade with the mages," she offered.

I had to remind her that automobiles don't rest; they break. We were stranded.

Lysandra, ever the optimist, suggested a stroll through the forest. "It will be charming," she said, though even she couldn't mask her unease.

"As long as no one trips and dies," Cerdan added with a nervous laugh.

We were all acutely aware of the danger lurking in these woods—the threat of wooden stakes, hidden among the trees, capable of ending our immortality in an instant.

And now Cerdan is trying to convince Alina to leave the carriage and walk through the forest home.

I plan to pretend the trip is one of Lady Yolanda's poise classes. Remember, Diary, she once made us walk through a room full of candles with books balanced on our heads. "Don't trip if you don't want to get burned," she said. It was a cruel but effective lesson, and one I might bring up to convince Alina to leave the safety of the car. After all, I don't want to spend any more time in the woods than we must.

Emma's Diary Entry

6th day of the Flower Moon, just after midnight

Dear Diary,

We finally made it home, and I'm barely keeping my eyes open as I write this. But I must get it all down before sleep steals these events from me.

Things grew... tense after we finally coaxed Alina out of the automobile. We're all alive—no one accidentally got staked—but there was a moment when it felt like that could change.

We hadn't even started walking when the air turned, cold tendrils wrapping around me like invisible chains. I froze, and the others stumbled into me with startled murmurs.

"Did anyone else feel that?" I asked, scanning the dark forest.

"Feel what?" Lysandra inquired, her earlier bravado waning slightly.

"Never mind," I said, dismissing it as a trick of the mind—until I saw her.

The Oracle of Shadows materialized from the gloom like a mirage born of the night itself, her silhouette barely distinguishable against the dark backdrop. A hood obscured her features, but the power emanating from her was unmistakable, ancient and profound. We all know *of* the Oracle—the being that knows all that was and will be—living in the forest to the south of us. But I've never come upon her before. No one knows why she settled here, rather than remaining with the fae and other non-human magical creatures in Avalaruin.

Lysandra gawked, Alina gasped, and Cerdan's eyes widened in both awe and fear. As for me, I stood rooted in place, my heart pounding wildly against my chest. The Oracle's reputation preceded her, a being of immense knowledge and foresight, her prophecies shaping the destinies of those she encounters.

"Travelers walking the path of twilight," she said, her voice a haunting melody, "step closer, child of the present, and glimpse your truth."

Despite my fear, curiosity pulled me forward. "Tell me, Oracle," I said, trying to sound bold.

"You seek what lies beyond your grasp, child of daylight," she murmured, her words weaving through the darkness like tendrils of mist.

Lysandra clung to my hand for support, and Alina's eyes darted nervously around us. Cerdan shifted uneasily, his usual confidence stripped away by the Oracle's cryptic words.

I tried to play it off with a smile. "Have no fear, Oracle. I'll stick to what's in my grasp—like my bed, which is where I plan to be as soon as possible."

But the Oracle wasn't finished. Her voice deepened as she spoke what sounded like a prophecy: "A path unseen, yet destined for your tread. Time weaves its threads around you, binding past and future in a dance of shadows."

And just like that, she vanished into the darkness, leaving me with nothing but the echo of

SHE WHO TURNS THE VAMPIRE

her words and a thousand unanswered questions burning inside me.

When the others asked if I was alright, I lied and pushed the strange encounter aside, vowing to deal with it later. I just needed to get us home.

Leaving the automobile behind, still seeping its last puffs of smoke into the night air, we picked our way through the underbrush, the crunch of dead leaves and cracked wooden sticks beneath our shoes a stark reminder of how vulnerable we were without the protection of steel. How vulnerable we all are when faced with prophecies delivered by creatures of the night.

It took hours, but I finally arrived home. When I nudged open the door to my chambers, the familiar scent of rosewater and parchment greeted me, a stark contrast to the wild earthiness of the forest we just escaped.

A glance at my desk revealed a neat stack of invitations and letters, undoubtedly left by Clara. Among them was an elegant envelope, thicker than the rest, sealed with the emblem of the Turned—an ornate 'T' intertwined with some kind of black flower and the initials L.M. On top was a note from Clara, written in her sharp hand.

"Emma," it read, "regardless of your willfulness, some obligations cannot be ignored. You are expected to meet with the Lord tomorrow evening after sunset. The Lord should not be kept waiting. And yes, I am aware you shirked your duties at the ball tonight."

I rolled my eyes at her attempt to scold me. The letters can wait until morning; my bed is calling. Let Clara cluck her tongue in disapproval tomorrow—right now, I'm too exhausted to care. What's one more night of rebellion against the looming threats and cryptic warnings from mysterious forest beings?

Sleep, at least, has no prophecies.

Mysterious Letter

Deliver the enclosed when the moment is ripe.

Emma's Diary Entry

6th day of the Flower Moon, morning

Dear Diary,

I've made it through all the letters but the most foreboding: the letter from the Turned leader, no doubt summoning me to some tedious meeting. I'm tempted to slip it into Demara's chambers and see what she makes of it. Let her deal with their endless demands. But it was the second to last letter that has me quickly jotting this down.

This morning arrived far too early, sunlight stabbing through the gauzy drapes and dragging me from dreams too muddled to recall. I groaned, stretching limbs that were tangled in sheets—and thoughts I'd rather not dwell on. When I finally rolled over, I saw my cluttered desk and was immediately reminded of the letters waiting for me. It seemed like they'd multiplied overnight, each one silently demanding my attention, as if the weight of responsibility could smother me entirely.

I finally dragged myself out of bed, weary limbs protesting as I shuffled to the desk. Nearly all the letters were a predictable assortment of social obligations and mundane demands. Lady Agatha had sent another invitation to one of her tiresome gatherings where Mr. Hawthorne will regale us—yet again—with his boar hunting escapade. We've vampires, literal predators, some of us may have even hunted humans, if I remember my lessons right. Mr. Hawthorne's 'talents' are simply a mage's spell on the lance.

Lady Agatha's invitation went into the "later" pile without a second thought. A demand for a meeting meant for Demara was quickly discarded, along with an unnecessary reminder from the apothecary. Only two letters remained—the one I'd been avoiding, and another, much plainer than the rest.

My fingers hesitated over that other envelope, an unremarkable thing that hardly seemed worth the effort. It was thinner and simpler than the others, standing out among its ornate counterparts like a daffodil in a field of roses.

I opened the plain letter, expecting little, and was right: it was a single sheet of paper folded in half. No signature graced its bottom, no flowery handwriting to squint at. Just a curt, block-written message:

"*Deliver the enclosed when the moment is ripe.*"

Frowning, I turned the note over in my hands, searching for some clue to its origin. But the paper was as nondescript as the words upon it.

And there was nothing else in the envelope—no signature, no further instructions. I turned the paper over again, searching for any clue about its origin, but found nothing. The mystery nagged at me as I held it, contemplating whether to simply toss it into the pile of forgotten correspondences. But then the parchment began to heat in my hand.

A sudden warmth spread across the paper, followed by thin wisps of smoke curling from its edges. I dropped it onto the desk as silver and gold tendrils spiraled into the air. The letter burned away in an instant, leaving nothing but ash—until a second, older letter materialized in its place.

It was ancient, yellowed with age, its edges curling like brittle autumn leaves. I ran my fingers over the paper, half-expecting it to crumble under my touch. But it remained intact, holding onto secrets from a time long gone.

The words on the front were written in an elegant, looping script: *"Critical but not urgent. Please open, _____."* The name was left blank, as if waiting for someone—perhaps me—to fill it in.

I slipped my finger under the sealed flap, attempting to pry it open. However, as soon as I touched it, the paper shimmered and emitted a soft light, remaining stubbornly sealed. The magic was powerful, and my curiosity piqued.

Whatever it is, Diary, it will have to wait.

Cerdan's standing reservation at Rye Lantern is calling, and with luck, I can slip away before Clara corners me about skipping the ball. I'm bringing the letter, I plan to ask Cerdan and Lysandra about it—perhaps one of them is behind it. We did talk about needing something to distract us lately. Or maybe... it's something more.

For now, the mystery remains, but at least it offers some intrigue.

Emma's Diary Entry

6th day after the Flower Moon (maybe?), evening

Dear Diary

Fates alive, I don't even know how to write this. Can you see my penmanship shaking?

It started—and remains—with that damned letter.

As planned, I took the letter to lunch, meeting Cerdan and the gang at Rye Lantern. So far, everything was normal. I was dressed to impress: hair coiffed just so, ruby red lips imparting a kiss of defiance, Diary in an interior pocket, and a lavender dress shimmering in the afternoon light, all perfectly complimenting the silver satchel at my hip. I won't even begin to describe what the dress—or my hair—looks like now.

Cerdan was at our usual table, bright blue eyes twinkling mischievously as he raised a toast in my direction. "I thought you might not make it after last night," he smirked, leaning back in his chair as I sat down next to him.

The usual scent of roasted coffee and sweet pastries filled the air, along with the exotic perfumes worn by the bar's eclectic clientele.

Even though it's been less than a day—I think—I already miss coffee.

Alina agreed with Cerdan, saying, "I almost didn't make it. My feet were killing me from all that walking."

"But you didn't really walk, did you?" Lysandra teased, winking at Cerdan. "You had the pleasure of being carried by our dear friend here."

"Because she promised to pay for my drinks," Cerdan joked, rolling his eyes.

Alina swirled her cup thoughtfully. "Emma should pay for all of our drinks after last night's drama with the auto and Oracle."

And I hadn't even been thinking of the Oracle, Diary, as the letter took up that mental space. "Speaking of drama," I said casually, toying with the edge of my satchel, the ancient letter nestled within. "I may have found something else to occupy our time."

Alina and Lysandra exchanged glances, and I went on, knowing I'd hooked them.

"It seems I have a secret admirer or a prankster on my hands," I announced, flashing the letter. The parchment gleamed in the warm light, edges scorched from its strange emergence.

Cerdan studied the aged paper with genuine surprise. "Old as the hills, it looks like."

"But first things first," I interrupted their speculation, looking pointedly at each of them. "Did any of you leave this for me?"

Lysandra grinned mischievously. "As much as I wish I had—we all know how much you detest receiving letters—I'm afraid not."

"Besides," Alina added, her gaze flitting back to the letter, "we were all too tired after last night to plot any secret deliveries."

SHE WHO TURNS THE VAMPIRE

"Then it seems we have a mystery on our hands," I declared, only half-joking. I attempted to open it again, more to show them what we were dealing with than in any hope that it would work. "It's not every day someone receives a letter that refuses to be read."

"Perhaps it's bewitched," Cerdan quipped, leaning forward with mock seriousness.

"Or cursed," Lysandra added with a theatrical glance over her shoulder. "Remember the Oracle's words last night? Something about 'a path unseen.'"

I laughed, the sound mingling with the clinking porcelain and distant hum of carriage wheels. "Yes, my answers must be found in cryptic correspondence. Clara will be thrilled."

"Maybe a mage sent it," Alina chimed in, her red curls bouncing. "Who wove spells into the paper?"

"Likely leading to a diplomatic incident," I replied dryly. "Which coven would risk the treaty with us just to send me a cursed letter?"

"There's no telling it was cursed," Cerdan said. Alina opened her mouth to retort, but he continued, "That's silly. It could just be something from a fae messenger," he suggested, his eyes speculative, "and simply misdelivered. Which is why the name isn't yet filled in."

"Could it be from a Turned?" Alina blurted out, trying to recover from Cerdan's implied insult. We all looked at her with raised eyebrows until she elaborated. "I know they aren't human anymore, but they were once. What if one didn't join a coven and instead became a vampire? They'd still have some magic, right? As a mage."

"True," I conceded, rolling the letter between my fingers, feeling the strange warmth of the parchment.

"Emma," Lysandra said, her voice taking on a note of concern, "do you feel alright? You look a bit pale."

That should have been my hint that something was awry, and I needed to toss the letter as far from me as I could. But it wasn't and I didn't.

"The mystery is getting to me, I suppose," I lied easily, trying to ignore the sudden dizziness that washed over me. A fleeting thought of danger crossed my mind, but I dismissed it just as quickly. Now I know I shouldn't have.

"Maybe you should let Clara take a look," Alina suggested, placing a reassuring hand on my arm. "She might know something about this sort of thing."

"Clara already has enough on her plate," I said with a grin, trying to shake off the lingering unease.

And the bright spots that appeared in my vision. "I'll manage, but thanks."

"You look as though you need some air," Cerdan said, reaching out as if to steady me. But before he could touch my hand, the world *lurched*. My breath hitched. My fingers clamped reflexively around the letter.

An icy breeze swept through the room, carrying the scent of rain-soaked cobblestones and the far-off echo of a bell tolling. My friends' voices faded, swallowed by an invisible tide.

"Emma?" Lysandra's voice sounded distant, panicked.

"Where did she go?" Alina's cry echoed from somewhere far away.

"Emma!"

But I was already gone. The ground vanished beneath my feet, replaced by a yawning abyss. The darkness swallowed me whole.

When I'm back home in my own bed, I'll write more of that feeling—that yawning mass of nothing. But I'm afraid if I do so now, I'll never stop writing.

I don't know how long I floated there, the darkness alive, shifting and breathing around me. My only tether was the letter, now glowing with an ethereal light that pulsed in time with my heartbeat. And then, without warning, the darkness burst into flames, and I into ashes.

When the world reformed around me, I stumbled, barely keeping my balance. Panic surged for a fleeting moment before I shook it off. Just another magical glitch in my day, surely?

But as I scanned my surroundings, Diary, a chill ran down my spine. I stood before a sprawling farmhouse, backed by a thick, dark forest. Wisps of smoke curled from the chimney, and a red barn—worn by time and weather—stood nearby.

My first thought, my first *hope*, was that the potion from yesterday had an exceptionally delayed effect. But no, I'd been transported. Transported to this... rural farm.

I glanced down at the letter still clutched in my hand. A name had appeared, scrawled in elegant handwriting: *William.*

I immediately wondered if this was where I was meant to find him. Did the letter send me to him?

Honestly, Diary, what kind of magic pulls me out of a perfectly nice cafe, plops me in front of a farmhouse, and then decides to play coy with details?

One thing's certain: I'm not anywhere near Fuil. The presence of wooden structures confirms that. In Fuil, wood hasn't been used in centuries—too much risk of splinters. We vampires prefer sturdier materials, things that won't kill us. But here? Here I am, in a place where wood is clearly still in fashion.

And no, I've not turned translucent or anything else, no other effects from the letter forthcoming—I checked. My skin remains as solid and golden as ever. But even now, as I sit in this empty barn, there remains this persistent... unease, as though something is watching me from the shadows.

The air is different here as well, colder. From the colors of the trees, I'd say I was in the midst of the Dispute Moon, after Lughnasadh. Instead of the actual season, only a week out from Beltane.

Still, this is bound to make for a *great* story at the next ball, isn't it? "Oh, just that time a mysterious letter whisked me off to a rural farmhouse."

Which leads me to what happened next.

I approached the farmhouse--

Emma's Diary Entry

6th day after the Flower Moon (maybe?), five minutes later

Apologies.

There was a sound outside the barn. I thought it was Lee's parents outside the barn, and I'm in no mood to take a stake to the gut today. As I was saying:

When I approached the farmhouse, I expected little from its worn, weathered exterior, and indeed, the inside offered no welcome surprises. The door, creaking on its rusted hinges, opened with ease, revealing an interior much like its façade—aged and neglected. Narrow beams of sunlight filtered through small, grimy windows, illuminating patches of the splintered and dusty floor.

I called out, my voice echoing in the silent space. I didn't expect an answer—who would want to live in such a place?—but it felt polite to ask.

I was about to explore further—away from potential splinters and the cobwebs clinging to the door frame—when a commotion shattered the stillness. Something heavy thumped against the ground, followed by the guttural snarls of a decidedly unfriendly creature.

Curiosity piqued, I hurried back outside to find a boy, likely no older than twelve, tearing out of the nearby forest, his face twisted with fear. Hot on his heels was a creature that resembled a dog, if dogs had six legs, a whip-like tail, and eyes that gleamed with a hunger that was almost desperate.

For a minute, I wondered if I'd been transported to Avalaruin instead of the Aboveground, where creatures like that lived with the fae and non-human beings.

"Ho there, ugly!" I shouted, infusing my voice with enough swagger to catch its attention. The creature jerked its head toward me, giving the boy the opening he needed to gain needed distance.

I spread my arms wide, projecting the power and confidence of a vampire—a predator far more dangerous than this strange beast. It hesitated, clicking its multiple legs against the ground as it sized me up. Dangerous as it was, I'm far deadlier. The boy stumbled to a halt, his wide eyes meeting mine, filled with a mix of fear and hope.

"Run!" I commanded, my voice cutting through the tension-laden air.

The boy didn't need telling twice. He bolted past me and through the open door, tripping slightly on the threshold before vanishing into the dim interior. The creature screeched, lunging at me, but I was quicker. With the grace of a dancer—thank you again, Lady Yolanda—I sidestepped its charge and delivered a swift kick to its side. It yelped, pride more wounded than its body, and scampered back into the woods.

Once I was certain it had fled, I followed the boy inside.

He was huddled in a corner, his small frame trembling as he clutched his fists tight. But as he saw me enter, relief washed over his features. He thanked me and I immediately asked if he was William.

But, alas, he shook his head, black hair flopping with the motion. "No, I'm Lee," he whispered.

(Which means my purpose here remains as mysterious as ever, Diary.)

"You're safe now, Lee," I told him, though inwardly I cursed my situation. I introduced myself, and asked, "Do you happen to know where the vampire settlement is? I should return before anyone notices I've gone."

His reaction was instantaneous—the blood drained from his face, and his eyes filled with the kind of fear that births nightmares. "V-vampire?" he stuttered, shrinking back.

I frowned, puzzled by his reaction. "Yes. Are we far from it?"

His expression remained tight, terror lingering like a storm cloud. "To the south, but you should never go that way," he finally managed to choke out.

But when I asked *why* I shouldn't go, his eyes darkened with something more than fear—something almost like anger. "Vampires are monsters," he said. "They cause pain and death."

Only the guards when they're protecting the border from non-monstrous hounds, I thought but didn't say. No use further scaring him. "Have you met any?" I asked instead.

He nodded, sharp and definitive.

There was a story behind that nod, one I was neither equipped nor particularly interested in uncovering after being yanked here without warning. I took a slow breath, trying to appear as non-threatening as possible.

"Lee, listen to me," I said, my voice steady. "There is nothing to be afraid of. Vampires aren't all bad."

He eyed me warily, still unconvinced. "How do you know?"

I *should* have probably weighed the risks, considered the consequences of revealing myself, but you know that isn't my style. "Because *I'm* a vampire," I said simply.

Lee's eyes widened, and he instinctively shielded himself, stumbling back until he hit the wall, looking at me with horror and disbelief.

"But I'm not here to harm you," I assured him. "In fact, I saved you from that creature out there, didn't I?" I offered a small smile, hoping to ease some of his tension.

His gaze flickered to the window, as though expecting the beast to return. "You... you did."

SHE WHO TURNS THE VAMPIRE

I rose, brushing the dust from my skirts, though the effort was pointless—my dress was well beyond saving after landing here on the ground. "And vampires aren't all bad. Some, perhaps. But no worse than humans." I glanced at him curiously. "You are human, aren't you?"

He nodded, this one not as intense as before. Just as he started to relax, a clatter outside made both of us freeze.

"That's my parents," he whispered urgently. "They can't see you. They'll try to kill you."

My eyebrows shot up. "Kill me?" I repeated, watching him scramble to his feet.

He nodded, glancing nervously toward the door. "My parents hate vampires. They think you're all monsters. They won't understand."

A child fearing what he doesn't understand is one thing, but adults? Surely they knew about the treaty. And truly, Diary, where are we that *doesn't*?

But the fear in his pale face said he believed it was a real risk.

I sighed. "Right. Well, before your parents come storming in with pitchforks, do you have somewhere... less rustic I can hide?" I glanced toward the barn out the grimy window and cringed. "Please don't say the barn."

His nod was swift, and before I could protest further, he tugged me outside towards that faeforsaken place.

I followed, not because I was scared of his parents, but because I needed more information. Home is south, he said, but how far? After last night, I'm not keen on a long trek back to Fuil. And if this community hates vampires... *everything* in the forest is a makeshift stake.

So, here I am, dear Diary, hiding in a barn. Cobwebs are everywhere, with dust thicker than I'd care to mention. It's everything I despise in one place. But I'm muttering under my breath about the indignity of it all alone. Lee's gone, forcing me to wait until his parents leave.

And while I wait? Well, I'm left wondering why the letter sent me here. To this dusty, disgusting barn. But I guess it'll have to wait until morning.

There had better be a prize at the end of this damned quest.

Emma's Diary Entry

7th day after the Flower Moon (maybe?), after midnight

Dear Diary,

I'm still here. And it's still night. But Lee's just left again.

When I awoke, Lee was standing over me with a lantern and a basket of food.

"Emma," he whispered, approaching cautiously, as if I might murder him for interrupting my slumber. "I brought you something to eat. Unless vampires don't eat." He scowled. "And I'm not offering myself!"

My lips twitched into a small smile at his newfound courage and defiance. "We eat food, but only for pleasure, not sustenance. Though if I stay here too long, I might need something else." I flashed a teasing bite in his direction, showing off my petite fangs.

The lantern wobbled, and he dropped the basket, his bravado fading. I winced inwardly—teasing a child who's clearly traumatized? Perhaps not my finest moment.

"Apologies," I said quickly, reaching out to steady the lantern. "That was a joke."

His expression softened as he knelt to gather the contents of the basket that had spilled. "It's okay," he mumbled.

I peeked at the offerings: bread, cheese, apples. More than I expected. I patted the ground beside me, inviting him to sit and thanked him. And then I did a little of the diplomacy Clara is always on about.

"You know," I told him, "where I live—in the vampire settlement—humans and vampires are friends."

Lee hesitated, but after a moment sat across from me, his eyes watching mine warily. "They don't kill us all?"

"Of course not," I said, biting into an apple. "There's a treaty, you know."

He nibbled at a piece of cheese, still holding it carefully in his small hands. "But... you drink blood?"

I chuckled softly, his curiosity now replacing the earlier fear. "Yes, but not in the way humans eat food. We don't hunt people or anything so dramatic." I leaned in and lowered my voice as if sharing a secret. "We drink animal blood, mainly. And we also have special donors, those who willingly share their blood, sometimes even in hopes of becoming vampires themselves."

Lee's eyes widened in disbelief. "You can become a vampire? You don't just... die?"

Of course, this is where Clara's lectures would have come in handy. Once I return home, I won't be telling her that her demand that I review my notes would have been helpful. But I cobbled together enough. "For about two hundred years now," I said, "because of a potion. But if a vampire drinks from an unwilling human, you just need to tell the Queen. Or the fae. The laws are strict against harming humans."

He stared at me for a long moment, something like hope flickering in his gaze. "Do you think I could visit? If there're nice vampires. And magic."

"Perhaps," I replied with a grin, "but you'd need a better reason than curiosity." Then, more serious, I asked, "But first, tell me about William. I'm supposed to deliver him a letter."

He frowned, puzzled. "No, no William that would have a letter from you."

I sighed, leaning back against the barn wall. "Then I have no idea why I ended up here. How far is the vampire settlement?"

"I don't know exactly," he admitted. "My parents and I moved here recently. It's quiet... no other children. But I'm learning about herbs and plants." His face brightened with that small confession. "I want to be a herbalist someday."

I smiled at his resolve. "A noble profession. The world needs more healers." Most herbalists were mages, though not all. Some had a command over magic without joining a coven. But coming from a family that feared vampires, they likely feared the unknown of magic as well. Perhaps that's why he's so curious about visiting the vampire settlement.

Lee looked down, a touch of sadness crossing his face. "My parents don't understand. They think it's a waste of time. They say I should learn to fight. Fight the vampires."

"Fighting's overrated," I said with a wink. "Plants don't try to kill you." A lie, if anyone had ever dealt with aconite or belladonna, but I doubted those were in his lessons yet.

He smiled faintly, then glanced at the barn door. "I should go. If my parents find out I'm here…"

I nodded. "I understand. Be careful."

And with that, Lee slipped out into the night, leaving the lantern behind.

Now, I am alone again. With the reception I'm getting, Clara needs to have a serious chat with Demara about managing her alliance with the humans. And keep me from having to play diplomat for her.

With the world outside still and silent, only now do I realize something odd—the farmhouse, the boy, everything feels strangely dreamlike, as if suspended in a reality not quite my own. Where in the world do people not know of the treaty? And who would fear us?

Maybe it's the lack of sleep. Or maybe I've stumbled into something far more complicated. Either way, I'm going back to sleep. When I wake, perhaps I'll find answers.

Or at the very least, a way back home.

Journal Entry of Lee Matthews

15th day of the Dispute Moon

EMMA'S GONE NOW.

Just like that—gone.

It felt like some weird dream, like it wasn't even real. She woke up before the sun, and we talked again. She didn't act like a vampire at all—not like the scary ones Ma and Da always warn me about. I wasn't even scared by the end. It was... different. I don't know how to explain it.

SHE WHO TURNS THE VAMPIRE 55

It all started last night. I brought her some food, even though I wasn't sure if vampires eat like we do. I brought bread, cheese, and apples. It seemed like the right thing to do, like maybe she'd like it. I mean, she saved me from the mordaire. She joked with me, saying something about needing blood if she stayed too long. I knew she was teasing, but it still made my heart pound. No one's ever teased me like that before. It was kinda weird, but also... nice?

It's hard to forget all the stuff Ma and Da say about vampires. How they're dangerous and would suck your blood in a heartbeat. But Emma... she wasn't like that. She was different. I didn't feel scared around her, not by the end.

She told me about this place where vampires and humans live together—like, as friends! She said they have a treaty, and there are people who give blood on purpose. Can you imagine that? I couldn't believe it at first. It's the opposite of everything I've been taught. Vampires are supposed to be monsters, right? Who would want to be friends with one?

I told her about my herbs, and she thought it was neat. She said herbalism was important and could help people. No one's ever said that to me before. Ma and Da think it's dumb. They want me to learn to fight and hate vampires. But Emma didn't laugh when I told her I wanted to be an herbalist. She said the world needs more healers.

No one's ever done that for me before. I think that's why I trusted her, why I wanted to show her the clearing. I took her there and showed her the herbs I'd been working on. She looked at them like they mattered. Like they were worth something. And when she told me I did a good job, I actually believed her. It felt really good, like someone finally heard me. She talked about how the peace treaty between vampires and humans started with herbs and potions, and that what I was doing had its own kind of magic. It felt like I wasn't just some odd boy who liked plants. What I was doing was real. And Emma made me believe that.

But then... everything went wrong.

We were standing there, just talking, when her face changed. It was like she wasn't really there anymore. Her body got all blurry, and her eyes went kind of distant, like she was being pulled away by something invisible. I reached out, called her name, but before I knew it, she just... disappeared. Right in front of me. One second she was there, and the next, she was gone. Like the wind had just carried her away.

SHE WHO TURNS THE VAMPIRE

I ran back to the barn, hoping maybe she'd come back. Maybe I'd imagined it, and she'd still be there, waiting. But no. It's just me now. Just the empty barn and the quiet woods. The lantern she left behind is still flickering on the ground.

I keep thinking about what she said. About that vampire settlement, where humans and vampires are friends. And now I can't help but wonder... what if Emma wasn't the only one? What if there are more vampires like her out there? What if everything I've been told is wrong? Maybe not all vampires are monsters. Maybe some of them are just... people.

And what if there are more people like Emma who think things like herbs are important? Who don't think it's dumb or pointless? It's an odd thought, but it kind of gives me hope. Hope that maybe there's a place where I fit in. Where what I care about matters.

But for now, I'm still here. And she's not. I don't know where she went or if she'll ever come back. I don't even know if she *can* come back, since she looked like she exploded or something. But I'll keep taking care of my herbs. It's all I can do.

Obituary

It is with profound grief that we announce the untimely passing of *W.M. Matthews* and his beloved wife, both of this parish, who met a most violent end at the hands of wicked and unnatural creatures. Their lives were cruelly cut short by the cursed race of vampires, whose vile predations have brought misery to this once-peaceful countryside.

Matthews was known for his unyielding strength and commitment to honest labor. His good lady wife, a woman of gentle demeanor and charitable spirit, was known for her kind-heartedness and grace. Their deaths have sent a shudder of horror through the town, and they shall be mourned deeply by all who knew them. Though their bodies have been taken from this world, the memory of their virtues shall remain a light in these dark times.

They leave behind their son, the younger Matthews. This parish hopes that those who can offer aid in this time of sorrow stand with him as he reckons with this most heinous crime.

May they find peace far from the horrors that took them from us.

Emma's Diary Entry

Unknown date, dawn

Dear Diary,

Fates, Diary, will I ever write an entry that doesn't sound fantastical and unbelievable again?

I'm—I'm still here. No, that's not true.

Of a sort.

I was pulled from Lee, from his charming little patch of herbs and the pride in his expression by the damn letter again. I know now it's the letter that's done it. The mechanism carrying out the Oracle's will, perhaps.

"Time weaves its threads around me," she'd said.

I'll weave my hands around the Oracle's neck the next time I see her, don't think I won't.

I was with Lee, when a familiar sensation washed over me, a tugging at the edges of my consciousness, pulling me away. The world around me started to blur. The clearing, Lee, his precious herbs—they all faded, slipping away as I was pulled from the peaceful forest and into the unknown once again. The last thing I heard was Lee's voice, faint and desperate, calling my name as I disappeared.

The world blinked into existence around me in a burst of color, and before I could even catch my breath, I stood in a different forest—a wilder, older cousin to the one I had just left. My head pounded with the force of the transport, as if the very act of moving had jarred my body and mind more severely than before. It was as if everything around me had shifted, but I was stuck, spinning in place. I'd assumed it was my head, but I know better now.

The letter did it, I thought then, assuming it brought me to this different forest when I failed to find William. Panic threatened to rise but I shoved it down. I told myself it was all just a silly little jaunt, one I'll be able to laugh over when I return home.

I'm not sure I'll be laughing now.

I took a deep breath, grounding myself, and began to walk, searching for something—anything—that might give me a clue as to where I ended up. The forest seemed impenetrable, with vines and roots tangling around my feet as I pushed forward. Then, like a mirage made of wood and age, an old barn materialized from the tangle of nature. Its weathered beams and sagging roof were almost familiar, a ghost of a memory from the barn where I spent the night Lee with. But this one looked... older. More rundown.

A shiver went down my spine, but before I could think too much about it, I heard movement behind me. A figure emerged from the trees, a boy no more than eighteen with long black hair, scowling wild-eyed with a pitchfork tightly gripped in his hands. His eyes were bruised, not from lack of sleep, but from a fight, and his lip, curled in anger, bled. He looked at me with such hatred, such suspicion, that my breath caught.

"Who are you?" His voice cracked like a whip through the stillness, demanding an answer. "What do you want here?"

I held up my hands, though nothing about me looked threatening though my instincts screamed at me to prepare to run. "I'm lost," I said, my voice as steady as it could be. "I don't mean any harm."

He didn't lower the pitchfork, brandishing it with a level of aggression that was both alarming and, under different circumstances, might have been comical. "Liar!" he spat, taking a step closer. "You're a vampire, aren't you? Where are the others? Where are your partners?"

I knew then I was still close to Lee's home, that I was still in danger in the community that hated me. But still, the accusation hit me like a punch to the gut. He knew what I was, but he was assuming the worst. "I'm alone," I said firmly. "And I'm not here to hurt you."

"Not here to hurt me?" His laugh was harsh and bitter. "Don't play dumb with me," he snapped. "I know a vampire when I see one. Where are the others? Your violent partners who like to carve up the innocent?"

My heart skipped a beat, not from fear but from the shock of his words. Vampires can't just roam around, killing indiscriminately. There are rules.

There's the treaty. But his pain was real. It was written in every tense muscle of his body.

"They should be in Demara's dungeon," I replied with a grim smile, hoping to disarm him with my sarcastic remark. I remember thinking—again—how apparent it was that Demara had issues with her reign, if so many in this community hated us.

How naïve I was.

"It's just me, myself, and I," I told the boy, "lost in these enchanting woods."

But my attempt at humor fell flat as the boy's expression twisted into something darker, something bitter. "Vampires like you took everything from me," he seethed. "My parents were murdered in cold blood."

My playfulness slipped away like water through my fingers. "I'm sorry," I said softly, the weight of his grief and anger cloying. "But I haven't hurt anyone. Vampires aren't allowed to kill humans. It's against the treaty."

"A treaty?" He practically snarled the word. "They drained my parents dry, and they enjoyed it." His voice trembled with emotion. "The ones who did it, roving bands of bloodthirsty monsters who kill and torture for fun. You're all the same."

SHE WHO TURNS THE VAMPIRE

"No!" I took a step back, my heart racing. "I'm not like them. I don't even know them." I was trying to piece this together, trying to understand how this could have happened. The treaty had been in place for centuries—vampires could only drink from willing donors. The rules were—are—*were* clear, and the consequences for breaking them were severe. But this boy's pain was real, his fear palpable.

He glared at me, black eyes narrowed, as if he's trying to see into my soul. "Why are you really here?" he demanded. "Why shouldn't I kill you right now?"

"William," I said, the name coming out more like a question than I intended. It rolled off my tongue, a plea. "Are you William?"

His gaze snapped to mine, suspicion etched into every line of his face. "How do you know that name?" His stance shifted, the threat of the pitchfork now secondary to the intrigue that sparked in his eyes.

"I was brought here with a letter. For William," I said, the words coming out rushed. I pulled the crumpled piece of parchment from my pocket, holding it out. "This letter. I don't know why, but it's important. I thought... maybe it was meant for you, that *it* is why I was brought here."

A shadow of grief flickered across his features before he caught himself. "William was my father," he said, his voice catching on the confession. His gaze dropped to the ground briefly before steeling again. "Now he's gone."

"Well, take it anyway and see," I said, extending my arm towards him. "It won't be opened by anyone but the true recipient, so there's no harm in you checking. And if I'm wrong, go ahead and kill me," I offered almost flippantly. Even knowing what I know how, I likely would have offered the same.

He took the letter, his eyes widening as he examined it. "This... this looks like my handwriting." He looked up at me, suspicion flaring again. "Why do you have a letter written in my hand? Are you some kind of vampire mage? A—a crossbreed?"

"No," I said with a sigh. "Magic is just nonsensical and inconvenient at times, that's all."

An understatement of the century, Diary. Of *all* the centuries.

A furrow formed between his brows as he flipped the letter over, examining the seal. "Magic you say?"

There was a hint of curiosity there, one that softened the harsh set of his mouth for a fleeting moment. Sliding a calloused finger under the edge, he cracked the seal, an audible flick slicing through the stillness.

"So you *are* William," I said in triumph and misguided relief.

"I am now, it seems," he said in a distant voice, more focused on examining the letter than on our conversation. "I was Liam, or Lee. Junior when times were good."

"Lee?" I echoed.

And then, it hit me like a lance to the brain. My eyes drew back to the building behind us, my gaze shifting to the trees, taller than they once were. The barn... *was* one I've seen before, just years earlier. The barn where I spent last night. *Or years ago.* "You're *Lee*?"

William's eyes widened as he scanned the letter, leaving me to stand there and wring my hands in anticipation. His gaze snapped up from the letter, locking onto mine with an intensity that stole my breath. "Yes," he confirmed.

Not just William, but Lee, Diary. Lee!

"And you're a time traveler," he said, his voice tinged with awe and dread. "You're... you're the vampire from my childhood."

Panic surged through me, and I staggered back, shaking my head. "No... this can't be possible."

I could barely process it, my thoughts spinning wildly.

Truthfully, I can still barely process it.

"I remember you," he murmured, almost to himself. Those piercing black eyes flicked back and forth between me and the letter, as if trying to make sense of something.

As he mumbled to himself, his nod seemed like a confirmation of some inner realization. "It's true. And you won't be my problem for much longer," he said, his tone oddly calm now. "The letter... it says how long you're staying. I wrote it to myself, in the future. From... the past."

"Because I'm going back home," I said, willing it into being. Time travel or no, I'd done what the letter demanded. I'd delivered it, I was sure there was no need for me to stay any longer.

Send me home.

But he looked up at me, his expression hardening again. "See you in twelve years, Emma."

Before I could protest or even comprehend what he meant, a ripple of magic coursed through the air, and the forest seemed to inhale sharply, the anticipation palpable. "Lee," I started, but the edges of my vision were already blurring, the world preparing to slip away again.

And then, with a final pulse of energy that crackled like lightning, I vanished. The whisper of leaves and the scent of pine were snatched away, replaced by a silence so profound it roared in my ears. Or perhaps it was just my own head filled with disbelief and dread at the realization that my journey through time was far from over.

The darkness rose. Yet again the last image burned into my mind is William—no, Liam, *Lee*—standing there, holding onto the letter with a mix of sorrow and resolve in his eyes as the forest faded away into nothingness.

Until—again, this was getting predictable, Diary—I was flung into solidness.

My body slammed into the ground with a thud, the impact knocking the wind out of me. Whatever unstained fabric of my lovely dress was destroyed by the muddy ground. I pushed myself up, spitting leaves from my mouth, an unpleasant reminder that the forest broke my fall. But it wasn't the forest I left behind. The trees stretched higher, older, more twisted than what I left.

Twelve years, Lee—Liam—said. Twelve years of what?

It's night again, though I can just see the dawn creeping through the trees. I'm sitting beneath a tree, trying to catch my breath, trying not to cry. A tightness creeps up my chest, squeezing the air out of my lungs.

This can't be happening. It doesn't make sense. Time travel? That's absurd. I'm not some character from a dusty novel. Time travel doesn't exist.

But, Diary, no matter how hard I try to rationalize, the forest around me is older. *Fates, I hope this is a different forest entirely.*

But somehow I know it isn't.

What kind of magic is this? Who could be behind it?

The world feels like it's closing in. But the forest remains indifferent, its ancient eyes watching me with quiet disdain.

I had to get this down. I had to write it out, try to make sense of it all before I'm whisked away again.

All that's left for me now is to dry my face and find Lee—Liam. And pray to the fates I'll be going home soon.

Emma's Diary Entry

The first day in this time, 6th day of the Dispute Moon (according to Liam)

Dear Diary,

I will be going home soon. Or "not long," according to my cantankerous host.

Right after my last entry, I picked myself up and set off in search of the dilapidated farmhouse. Liam said twelve years would pass before I saw him again, and certainly, the place wouldn't have improved in the meantime.

As I wandered the woods, trying to find something familiar—a path, a landmark that would lead me back to Liam—a voice cut through my spiraling thoughts, cold and dripping with venom.

"Emma."

I whipped around, and there he stood: tall, lean, with long black hair and dark, intense eyes. But it wasn't the bloody young man I had met minutes ago, armed with a pitchfork and blazing with fury. Nor was it the fearful child who had offered me refuge in his home. No, this was a man—older, sharper—but still, recognition rippled through me. This was Liam as I am, an adult. (Although with that ever-present glower, it won't just be my immortality that leaves me looking younger than him as time passes.)

"Emma," he repeated, clearly irritated by my prolonged stare. He made my name sound more like an accusation than a greeting.

"Lee—Liam?" I took a step closer, blinking up at him, trying to reconcile the familiarity of his face with the changes I saw. "You—"

"Thirty," he interrupted, folding his arms across his chest, as if daring me to question it. "You're supposed to show up when I'm thirty. And here you are." His lips curled into a sneer, his voice bitter. He had been waiting for this, dreading it, and yet, as he said... here we were.

Even though I knew the truth, I couldn't help but deny it. "No," I whispered, shaking my head as if I could dispel reality. "This isn't real." My heart pounded. I tried to breathe, to force some calm into my racing thoughts, but the panic only grew.

But it was real then, just as it is real now as I sit inside his stuffy house.

And Liam—older, hardened, and far more bitter than the teenager I met hours earlier—stared at me with the cold, calculating eyes of a man who'd been long acquainted with disappointment.

"You don't believe it," he said, almost mockingly. "But you will."

"I have to get back," I urged. "There must be a way to reverse this."

He tilted his head, his gaze sliding over me as if he was assessing a particularly unpleasant insect. "Let me spare you the trouble. You can't. You're stuck here. For now."

"No," I said, as if repeating it would make it true. "No, I don't belong here. I need to get back to Fuil. I—" My voice faltered as reality set in, the weight of it crushing. "You said you wrote yourself the letter, telling you how long I'd be here."

"I knew you'd be here," he snapped. There was venom in his tone, but beneath it, exhaustion. Like he'd been bearing the impact of my arrival, dreading the inevitable disruption. "I didn't know precisely when, of course," he added, his voice laced with bitter sarcasm. "But your timing, as always, is impeccable."

The hostility in his tone had me almost remind him of my timing when he was a child, when he needed saving from that odd dog-creature. But the overwhelming disbelief at the current situation kept me quiet. "What do you mean?" I asked. "What's happening?"

"What's happening?" His tone turned mocking, dripping with barely contained malice. "Oh, you're curious now, are you?" He let out a soft, humorless laugh. "What's happening is unchecked aggression from your kind. The northern bands of vampires—quite charming, really—are becoming... feral, if you can imagine. The Fae are in a frenzy, but they don't dare move against the vampires just yet. No, too much politics, too many agreements conveniently keeping them at bay while your kin continue their delightful rampage. The humans, predictably, are dying in droves while the immortals waste their time."

My stomach churned. "But the treaty between vampires and humans—"

"There is no treaty!" he spat. "They don't care about laws or peace. They want blood. They take what they want and leave bodies in their wake."

The memory of the night I spent in his barn offered little insight into this world. It could have been a rural outpost for all I knew; there was nothing to tell me I'd time traveled. Only now do I realize it could have been *anywhere* in the past. I sifted through my memories desperately trying to piece everything together. How far back, I'm not sure.

The Treaty came after the potion, perhaps decades later if I remember right. (Damnit, Diary, yet again I wish I'd read my notes as Clara demanded.) It took time for the fae to feel comfortable that the potion worked, and gather support to cull out the vampire naysayers. My family came into power that way, a distant cousin dying and my line affirming the treaty and playing nice with the humans and the newly Turned. With no treaty, I must be *at least* a hundred years in the past.

I can hardly believe it to even write it here, Diary. It just didn't make sense.

"I can't just... stay here," I told my irritated host. The words came out weaker than I intended, and I hated how small I sounded.

Liam's eyes flashed with impatience. "I suppose I must be the one to inform you that the world does not, in fact, revolve around your precious needs."

I know that because if it were true, I wouldn't be here at all, I thought mutinously.

"The letter. How long am I staying this time?" I finally asked, breaking the heavy silence between us.

Liam's face darkened, and his eyes narrowed as he looked me up and down. "Not long," he said, sneering again. "But, unfortunately, long enough to be my problem. Because, as luck would have it, I'm the idiot who thought it wise to write myself that infernal letter. So now, thanks to my past self's infinite wisdom, I'm saddled with you."

I arched an eyebrow, panic forgotten in light of his derision. "You are?"

"Unfortunately, yes," he replied, cold as ice. "I knew this day would come, so I prepared. And now here you are, again, and what do you expect me to do? Simply let you wander off into the woods to be torn apart? Or worse?" His voice lowered dangerously on the last word.

I crossed my arms, irritation bubbling up despite the circumstances. "You could," I replied, the petulance easily rising. "I am a vampire." I may not have done much fighting or training or—I won't number my faults today, Diary, I am far too tired—but my fangs remain deadly.

Liam's eyes narrowed dangerously. "Don't you dare use that as a bargaining chip with me," he hissed, the venom in his voice poisoning the tension between us. "I have seen firsthand what vampires are capable of. You cannot cry foul and claim your innocence as a species in one breath and try to intimidate me in another."

I held his gaze, the weight of his words settling around us like a heavy cloak. Despite the defiance that simmered within me—an emotion to drown out the fear and panic—I couldn't deny the truth in his eyes. There was a weariness there, a deep-rooted resentment borne from years of witnessing the darker side of my kind. How many lives had been torn asunder by vampires in this world I found myself in? That he was even letting me stay in his presence was something I couldn't take for granted.

That I *can't* take for granted, Diary, no matter how much I'd like to.

"Fine," I said, my voice firmer now. "If I can't go back, then I'll stay—for now." Straightening my posture, I tried to project some semblance of composure despite the dirt on my dress and the leftover anxiety in my chest. "Thank you for your hospitality."

He grumbled something under his breath before grabbing me by the arm and tugging me toward his shabby-looking house, which looks even more rundown than it did... years ago. "Inside. Now."

I barely managed to keep my feet under me as he pulled me along, shoving me through the front door and slamming it behind us.

But the interior of his house was starkly different from the brief glimpse I previously had.

Gone were the bare walls and dusty shelves, replaced with a chaotic yet organized display of books, jars of herbs and potions, and vials of mysterious liquids. There was a workbench littered with tools, and an enormous cauldron bubbling quietly in the corner.

"You became a herbalist?" I asked tentatively.

"A healer," he corrected sharply, moving to one of the shelves and pulling down a jar with an irritated flick of his wrist. "Yes, I use herbs, but don't delude yourself into thinking I spend my days frolicking through meadows with a basket of flowers."

I blinked at him, remembering Lee showing me his collection of "flowers" with such fondness. "Why not join a coven? You could have left all this behind."

With no parents and nothing tying him here, he could surely have left what must be a place full of terrible memories.

He turned to me, an exasperated look on his face. "Because," he drawled, as if speaking to a particularly dull child, "I have no interest in shackling myself to a coven and subjecting myself to their... insufferable doctrines. I value my freedom far too much to spend my life surrounded by people who think they know better."

"So you live alone out here?"

"Yes," he replied shortly. "I'm hardly the town darling, if that wasn't abundantly clear. My childhood delight for vampires made me quite the pariah—something that was beaten out of me by the soldiers when my parents were murdered." He flashed me another scowl, as though it was my fault.

Diary, his parents death is not something he can blame me for, surely? They were already enemies to vampires. But perhaps my rather carefree comments about vampire and human relationships—which I likely wouldn't have said had I known I was in a different time period... possibly—may have given him the wrong idea. Particularly in a world as violent as he's described. I should have chosen my words more carefully years ago—but how was I to know I'd end up in the past?

I couldn't think of how to respond to his claim, but he didn't appear to be waiting for one. He continued, "but it suits me just fine. And no one will come for you."

I let the silence hang before forcing some strength into my voice. "You don't need to take care of me, you know. While I appreciate a place to stay, although I will complain if I'm meant to sleep in that barn again." I shook my head, flinging away memories of sleeping on the ground. "I'm sure twenty years hasn't made it any more comfortable. But I'm perfectly capable of—"

"Of what?" he interrupted, his voice rising. "Surviving? In this world? Do you even understand what's going on out there?"

I straightened my back. "I—"

But he wasn't done. His sneer returned, sharp and cruel. "You've barely scratched the surface of the danger out there. And now you expect me to let you traipse off into the wilderness as if it's a merry stroll through the park?" He turned his back on me, focusing on his workbench, his movements sharp and precise. "You stay here," he ordered coldly. "Do as I say, and perhaps—just perhaps—we'll survive long enough for you to vanish from my life once more."

There was a heaviness in his words that cut through me, a burden he carried that I hadn't fully understood. My heart sank with the weight of it, and a pang of guilt twisted in my chest. Neither of us asked for this, yet here we are.

Panic still thrummed beneath the surface, but it was muted now by the stark reality of my situation. I sank into one of the old chairs by the fire, its warmth doing little to ease the icy knot in my stomach. "You know," I said quietly, "it's not my fault."

Liam sighed wearily, rubbing a hand over his face. "I know," he said, his voice softer now, almost resigned. "I know. But it doesn't make it less unbearable."

And in that, he's right.

Journal Entry of Liam Matthews

8th day of the Dispute Moon, 1695

She's here.

Emma. Twelve years passed, and she's here again, just as the letter said she would be. *But why?*

I don't understand it—don't understand her. What in the faes' names possessed my future self to saddle me with this—*this*—creature? A vampire. Of all things. The single happy moment in time with her from my childhood doesn't overcome decades of baggage.

She is going to upend your life. She will irritate you beyond measure.

I'd written that to myself, along with varying other sentiments.

At least she won't be here long.

Good.

She doesn't belong here. I don't want her here.

Why did I write that letter?

Thirty years old, cantankerous and alone, and this is what it all comes to? Waiting for some lackadaisical vampire to waltz back into my life with no answers, no explanation, just confusion and *arrogance*?

I knew it was coming, I knew it, and yet I—

I still don't know what to do.

Why is she here?

When will my life be mine again? When will I be alone again?

Emma's Diary Entry

12th day of the Dispute Moon, unknown year

Dear Diary,

Liam's house is impossibly small. Not physically, of course—it's certainly large enough for one person to live comfortably. But for two people, especially two people who seem to agree on *nothing*, it feels suffocating.

He remains in his childhood bedroom, and I reluctantly occupy his parents' old bedroom. It's slightly morbid, their clothes and things still present as a somber reminder of their absence, and smells of mothballs, but it's still better than the barn. The old bed—squeaky as it is—has its charms, if you ignore the fact that it probably hasn't been slept in for more than a decade. The blankets are scratchy, the floors creak with every step, but I've made peace with the spiders that have taken up residence in the corners. It is much better waking up with dirt in my hair and bugs burrowing in my clothes.

Earlier this morning I was stretched out lazily in one of the rickety old chairs by the fire, twirling a strand of my hair around my finger as I watched Liam shuffle around his workbench. He's always in motion, always *doing* something—grinding herbs, boiling concoctions, muttering incantations under his breath. The only time he isn't glowering at me is when he's too busy focusing on whatever potion he's concocting. And at least at *first*, I preferred it that way. Better he leave me alone, better I not be sneered at *all* day.

But eventually, even that became preferable to the monotony of our days together.

"What *are* you doing?" I asked, more out of sheer boredom than genuine curiosity. By day three, I'd run out of things to entertain myself with, and I started feeling like I might just climb the walls if something didn't change.

He didn't even glance at me. "Work," he said, voice dripping with that familiar disdain, as if I'd asked him something utterly stupid. Which, knowing him, he probably thought I had.

"Yes, but what kind of work, Mr. healer-herbalist?" I pressed. "Potions? Hexes? Curing the village of their collective misery?"

He paused for a moment, then fixed me with a look that could melt stone. "If you must know," he drawled with a sneer, "I'm preparing the last of the tinctures to sell in town tomorrow. Not that it concerns you in the slightest."

Town. My ears perked up. "You're going to town?"

"Yes," he replied cautiously, as though regretting every word. "I do have a livelihood to maintain."

I sat up. "Then I'm coming with you."

His eyes widened for a brief second before his frown deepened into a full scowl. "You most certainly are not."

"Come now," I said, standing up and moving closer to him. "I've been cooped up in this house for *days*, Liam. I'm bored out of my mind. You can't possibly expect me to just sit here forever."

"I can, and I do expect you to remain until I'm finally relieved of your presence," he replied sharply. "The last thing I need is you traipsing around, drawing attention to yourself and, by extension, to me."

"I won't draw attention," I insisted, smiling sweetly to soften his stubbornness. "I'll wear something plain—one of your mother's old dresses, perhaps. And a hat. No one will even notice me."

He crossed his arms, giving me a long, skeptical look. "Do you truly think a dress and hat will conceal the fact that you're a vampire?"

I shrugged. "Why not? I'll stay covered, stay out of the sun, keep to the shadows. Besides, I'm perfectly capable of blending in when necessary."

Liam scoffed. "Blending in? You?" His laughter was as bitter as the herbs he ground. "You'll get yourself killed. Or worse, you'll get *me* killed."

"You're being dramatic," I told him. "I'm not as helpless as you seem to think I am."

"You think so?" he said, not even bothering to look at me as he ground herbs with a pestle.

The sharp scent of crushed plants and earth filled the surrounding air. It's starting to remind me of Liam, his earthy scent. "You couldn't even manage to boil water without burning half my kitchen down. How do you expect to survive a trip to town when they all want to kill you?"

I flushed slightly at the reminder of my earlier mishap (I *may* have under-described what happened in my entry earlier in the week, Diary), but I refused to back down. "I'm not asking to start a war, Liam. I just want to get out for a bit. See the world. Find out what year it is—maybe even enjoy myself."

He slammed the pestle down harder than necessary, finally turning to face me fully. "This is not your world to enjoy, Emma," he snapped, his voice dripping with that usual haughty disdain. "It's dangerous. Unpredictable. And I, for one, have no interest in carting you around like some fragile, useless doll."

I nearly bit back a retort but stopped myself. He was right, in his own infuriating way. Still, Diary, I couldn't stay cooped up in this house forever. I needed to see what was out there, needed to get a sense of how far back in time I've ended up and what has changed. Maybe if I could understand this world better, I could find a way back to my own time.

I took a deep breath and softened my tone. "Liam, please. I'll stay hidden, I promise. I won't be a burden. But I need to get out of here."

He eyed me for a long moment, his lips curling into a sneer. "I'll regret this," he muttered darkly. "Mark my words."

I grinned at him, satisfied. "You won't regret a thing."

We're leaving within the hour and I'll check in. Here's hoping I don't start a riot in the town!

Emma's Diary Entry

12th day of the Dispute Moon, unknown year, evening

Dear Diary,

It isn't Fuil. It isn't even Bec. It's a rural town no more than a relic from centuries past—because it *is*. There was no hum of electricity, no semblance of modernity, and nothing but dirt roads and ramshackle buildings. The air was thick with the smell of sweat, earth, and something foul I can't quite place. It wasn't even charming in an old-fashioned way; it was simply... desolate.

Before traveling to the miserable excuse for a town, I wrapped myself into one of his mother's old dresses—a plain, drab thing in a muted brown—and a wide-brimmed hat that hid most of my face. The dress was too long, pooling at my feet and the hat smelled faintly of dust. I felt ridiculous, but if it meant getting out of the house, I was willing to endure it.

Liam was less than pleased. He kept glancing at me on the walk from his farm to town, his brows furrowed as if waiting for me to do something catastrophically stupid, his shoulders hunched, clearly bracing himself for the inevitable disaster he was convinced would occur.

"You look like an oversized child playing dress-up," he grumbled under his breath as we made our way through the outskirts of town.

"Charming, as always," I replied, adjusting the hat slightly to better shield my face from the townspeople and his disapproving glare. "You're just jealous that I make even this dreadful thing look good."

He scoffed, but said nothing more as we passed through the narrow streets lined with ramshackle buildings. It has been so long since I'd seen a town like this: old, insular, and unwelcoming. The townspeople walked about with their heads down, avoiding eye contact. They moved like ghosts, haunted by lives that seem to extend no farther than these dilapidated buildings.

I could see Liam's unease too. Every sideways glance or murmur seemed to set him more on edge.

He led me to a small marketplace where he set up his stall. He unloaded his tinctures and potions with practiced efficiency, all while giving me occasional glares as if daring me to do something reckless. I stood off to the side, watching him with mild interest while trying to get a better sense of my surroundings.

"You know, if you keep scowling like that, your face might freeze that way," I quipped. He shot me another withering look, but there was a hint of amusement dancing at the corners of his lips. It was a small victory, but one that made my heart flutter inexplicably. I hadn't seen him smile since I arrived. It blossomed across his face, smoothing out the ever-present anger lines into something soft and pleasing.

Encouraged by my tiny triumph (and, to be honest, needing to get away from the odd feelings Liam's smile invoked), I ventured further from the stall, letting my curiosity lead me to the edge of an-

SHE WHO TURNS THE VAMPIRE

other stall selling strange trinkets—carved bones, vials of dark liquid, little bits of jewelry that look like they had seen better days. Two women stood just a few feet away, speaking in hushed tones. The merchant was busy arguing with a customer over the price of a necklace, and I took the opportunity to listen in on the women's nearby conversation.

"Did you hear? The fae are demanding *another* meeting about the vampire problem," one woman said, her voice low.

My ears perked up, and I subtly inched closer while pretending to examine an old bottle displayed on a nearby shelf.

The other woman scoffed. "About time. Those creatures are getting bolder every day. My cousin's farm was attacked last week. They barely made it out alive."

"Someone ought to do something," the first woman said, shaking her head. "The fae won't stand for it much longer. They'll remove them all if the vampires don't come up with a solution. Though why the fae would even give them a chance is a shock to me."

Remove them? I couldn't believe it. Surely the fae wouldn't...but I remembered snippets of Clara's history lessons, and how, exactly, the fae became the ruling species in Avalaruin.

"Excuse me," I said, turning toward the women with what I hoped was a friendly smile. "I couldn't help but overhear. I'm new in town... What's this about a vampire problem?"

The first woman, her green eyes wary and calculated, measured me up for a moment before speaking. "You must be new to the *world* if you don't know about the Aislean," she said, her tone cautious but curious.

"Aislean?" I repeated, feigning ignorance.

"They're the vampires," the second woman explained. "They were born as such, able to walk in daylight, live for centuries, and drink human blood like it's water. Lately, they've been wreaking havoc and attacking humans like the monsters they are."

I swallowed hard. This wasn't the world I knew. Not even close.

"But," I started slowly, trying to piece it all together, "I've heard stories of humans *becoming* vampires, protecting the humans from death... isn't there some sort of potion that can—"

The first woman scoffed, cutting me off mid-sentence. "Potion? No, love. There's no such thing. The Aislean would never allow that. If a human were to be turned into one of them, it'd be a disaster. There's already enough tension between the vampires and the rest of us, and the fae wouldn't stand for it."

The second woman nodded grimly. "It's bad enough that the Aislean exist at all. If they start turning humans into more of them... well, I'm certain the fae High King would destroy them without hesitation."

My stomach dropped. No turning potion. No way for humans to become vampires. That potion doesn't exist yet, which means...

I'm at least two hundred years in the past, Diary. Maybe even more.

Standing there, by that blasted stall with those irritating women, panic threatened to bubble up inside me, but I forced it down, swallowing the knot in my throat. I couldn't afford to react in front of those strangers. I needed to stay calm, to figure this out. Surely there is a way back, I thought to myself, all the better to calm myself down. *There has to be.*

Before I could dwell too much on that terrifying thought, the conversation shifted again.

"Of course, it would be easier if we had any competent healers around here," the first woman grumbled with a huff. "Do yourself a favor, young lady, and try not to get injured."

"I thought there was a healer," I said faintly, still reeling from my inadvertent discovery.

"Oh, him," the second said with a disdainful sniff. "He's nothing but trouble. Always skulking about, keeping to himself. Worthless, truly."

"He's dangerous, if you ask me," the first woman concluded with a shudder. "It's best to avoid him at all costs."

I took a deep breath, fighting the urge to snap at them. I don't know why my hackles raised so quickly. But I couldn't just let them talk about him like that, Diary. I couldn't.

"Well," I said, stepping forward with a bright smile that didn't reach my eyes, "I guess it's a good thing I'm not asking your opinion of him."

Both women blinked in surprise at my sudden boldness. I didn't give them a chance to respond. Instead, I pivoted on my heel and marched back towards Liam's stall, my heart pounding in my chest.

Just in time to see a burly man looming over him, clearly spoiling for a fight.

"You again," the man said. He was broad-shouldered and rough-looking, with a permanent scowl etched into his face. "Selling your little mage brews, are ya?"

Liam stiffened but didn't look up. "I'm selling remedies," he said coldly. "If you have no need for them, move along."

The man sneered. "Remedies, sure. More like poison. Why don't you take your cursed potions and shove 'em up—"

"That's enough," I said, stepping forward before I could think better of it. "He's trying to make a living."

The man's eyes widened in surprise as he looked at me, then narrowed as he took in my appearance. "And who might you be? Some worthless apprentice?"

"None of your business," I replied coolly. "Now, unless you're buying something, I suggest you keep moving."

He stepped closer, looming over me with a malicious grin. "I'm just having a bit of fun. No need to get all riled up, little lady."

"Step back," I hissed, tilting my chin up defiantly. "Or else you may find yourself on the wrong end of one of these so-called poisons."

Liam's gaze was surely burning into me from behind but I ignored him. It was reckless, yes, but I couldn't help it. Perhaps because, Diary, in some small way, I feel responsible for him—just as he's responsible for me.

And that man was nothing but a bully, and I wasn't about to let him ruin my first day out of that damned house. Not more than the revelation that I'm two centuries in the past already had.

He hesitated for a moment, studying me with confused eyes before grumbling something under his breath and storming off.

I exhaled slowly, the tension in my shoulders easing. Liam was watching me with a strange expression—something between surprise and... respect?

"Eavesdropping is such an unbecoming trait, Emma," Liam said finally. "You really should learn some restraint."

I shrugged nonchalantly. "He was being a nuisance."

"You may have revealed yourself as a vampire," he pointed out with a raised eyebrow.

I grinned, unable to resist teasing him. "Well, at least now people will stop bothering you if they think you have a pet vampire protecting you."

He huffed, half-amused, half-exasperated. "Pet vampire, indeed," he grumbled, but there was a slight twitch at the corner of his lips. Although this expression didn't pool heat in my belly like the first had.

"Maybe that's why the letter has continued to keep me here," I mused aloud, trying to make sense of my strange situation. "Defending dashing chemists from burly troublemakers."

I heard him make a surprised sound, but I was too busy closing my eyes, hoping that saying it out loud would trigger something. Because maybe that was why I was still here, to defend him. That maybe I'd be pulled back to my own time. But when I opened them again, nothing had changed. I was still here.

And whatever emotions I thought I saw in Liam's expression a moment ago were gone, replaced by something else, something I couldn't decipher. Something that *did* make my stomach clench.

Emma's Diary Entry

16th day of the Dispute Moon, unknown year

Dear Diary,

I've thrown myself into figuring out, exactly, when I had arrived.

After the encounter in town, with the news that the turning potion didn't yet exist, the tense talk of vampire problems and the demand for fae to exterminate us, I can't shake the gnawing uncertainty inside me. I need to know the exact year, the political climate, and most importantly, if there is any hope of returning to my own era. If saving Liam isn't what's bound me to this time, there must be something else...

20TH DAY OF THE DISPUTE MOON · AB YEAR 169

THE LATHA SPECTATOR

TIDES OF BLOOD

LOCAL AUTHORITIES ACROSS LATHA HAVE REPORTED A DISTURBING INCREASE IN THE VAMPIRIC DEATH TOLL.
IN RESPONSE TO THE CRISIS, CITY COUNCILS HAVE INITIATED MEASURES TO COMBAT THE MENACE, INCLUDING INCREASED PATROLS DURING THE NIGHT AND THE ESTABLISHMENT OF SAFE HAVENS FOR THOSE AT RISK.
ADDITIONALLY, A HEIGHTENED FOCUS ON PUBLIC AWARENESS AND EDUCATION REGARDING VAMPIRE WEAKNESSES AND PREVENTION STRATEGIES HAS BEEN URGED TO AID IN MINIMIZING FURTHER CASUALTIES.

LEADERS CALL FOR THE FAE TO INTERVENE BEFORE IT IS TOO LATE.

Emma's Diary Entry

29th day of the Dispute Moon, unknown year

Dear Diary,

The town has nothing that amounted to a library. Though, to be fair, I don't know if Fuil does either, besides The castle's records room. Instead, I've been spending countless hours poring over whatever scraps of information I could find in Liam's small, cluttered home. Not that there is much to begin with. Liam has no interest in non-magical or non-herbology books, and his family didn't keep records of historical events. My only resources are my memory of vampire history and occasional snippets from eavesdropping on the townsfolk when we go into town.

I can only imagine how furious Clara will be with me, if she realizes how valuable her lessons could have been, had I remembered them better. I'm close to throwing a fit myself.

But even with the ghost of Clara's lessons in my head, I don't know enough about humans to distinguish how far in the past I am. At least two hundred years, but could it be more? In my time, humans have had electricity for quite some time, but they've only recently invented automobiles. Without magic, they must find other means to entertain themselves.

But Liam's town is backwards and more rural than any I've seen, like some of the stories of those northern human outposts, the fishing settlements. If not for my realization of the missing turning potion, I still could have thought I was *somewhat* near my time...

Diary entry of Jane Matthews

1st day of the Ice Moon; *Imbolc, 1665*

I WRITE TODAY WITH trembling hands, for the world has changed in ways I could not have imagined. He is here. My son. A tiny thing, so fragile and pink, but already he feels like the weight of the world. Born on Imbolc, the day of light returning, a day of renewal. Some say children born on this day are destined for great things—or perhaps drawn to dark paths. I shudder to think what that could mean for him in a world filled with shadows.

They tell me I should name him William, after his father—after the man who stares at me with those cold eyes, expecting me to shape our son in his likeness.

But in my heart... I do not want another William. No. This child is not just his father's son. He is mine. I will call him Liam, though William insists I do otherwise.

The night was long, and the pain nearly unbearable. I fear the shadows more than ever, for I know what lurks beyond the light of our hearth. The midwives whispered of bloodsuckers haunting the hills, of dark things that prowl in the night. And I wonder—will Liam grow to fear them, too? Or will he become one of the brave men who guard this land from such evils?

Emma's Diary Entry

5th day of the Harvest Moon, 1695

Dear Diary,

I finally know when I am.

This morning I stumbled upon an old half-burnt journal wedged between two floorboards in Liam's parents' bedroom. Taking it to the study, I brushed off the dust, revealing faded ink labeling it as "Jane's."

Just as I was about to dive into its pages, Liam appeared at the doorway, a satchel of tinctures slung over his shoulder, ready for another trip to town. His eyes flicked down to the journal in my hands warily.

"Did you find something interesting?" he asked, his tone neutral but not unkind. A change from the sharp, clipped tone he used when we first met. He's softened these past few weeks—his sharp tongue dulled, and the glares that once burned with disdain are more like passing annoyances when I interrupt him rather than full-fledged scorn.

When I first arrived, we moved around each other cautiously, like strangers in a cramped room. Now, though, we've developed an easy rhythm, navigating his cluttered home and the surrounding woods that feels almost practiced. I step aside when I see him coming, and he silently hands me things I need before I even ask for them. He even brought home a bucket of pig's blood from the butcher for me when I needed it. It's nothing *extraordinary* or life-changing, but it feels like... something.

To his question, I answered, "A journal."

Liam set his tinctures down and glanced at the journal with a mix of nostalgia and something like dread. "It belonged to my mother," he said dismissively. "It's probably useless."

I stood, meeting him at the doorway. "You never know," I said with forced optimism. Because one of us needed to hold on to hope. "Who knows what secrets could be in here?"

Liam arched an eyebrow, his skepticism clear as he regarded me with a sideways glance. "Secrets? In my mother's journal?" A ghost of a smile touched his features. "You have quite the imagination, my dear."

The endearment caught me off guard, a warm flutter dancing in my chest at the sound of it. Liam, too, seemed to realize what he said, and a faint blush crept across his cheeks. Clearing his throat awkwardly, he grumbled, "Do you need anything from the market?"

I shook my head, and he hurried off, leaving me alone with Jane's journal.

Once he was gone, I flipped through the brittle pages, piecing together the entries as best I could. The ink was faded, the handwriting cramped and uneven, but I found what I needed. Jane's last dated entry was just after Liam's birth—putting me 214 years before my own time.

214 years, Diary! How much danger am I really in here? Were we hunted first, like that woman from the market hinted?

Did the fae *try* to destroy us before that mage finally invented the potion? The fae are notoriously powerful and unpredictable, capable of great magic and great cruelty. They gave us our land, when we sided with them during the Great War thousands of years ago. They could take it—and our lives—away with the snap of a finger.

[Clara, if you ever find this journal, I promise I'll never take your lessons for granted again.]

By the time Liam returned, I had spent hours trying to reconcile everything. I was sitting by the fire when he found me, his usual mask of indifference softening as he asked, "Find anything useful?"

"A bit," I replied, setting the journal down gently beside me. "I've narrowed down the year. I'm 214 years in the past."

"That far back?" he murmured, his brow furrowing in thought.

"Yes, Jane's last entry coincides with your birth year. It all adds up." I sighed, rubbing my temples.

"I hadn't realized that was what you were searching for," he said, looking almost guilty, if his face had enough emotion to create the expression. "You could have asked me the year."

I sucked in a breath, unsure whether to chastise him or myself. Why hadn't he just volunteered the information, or asked what I was researching? Did I have to spell everything out for him? Instead, I let the irritation fade, reminding myself that Liam has been living alone for a long time now. It isn't as though I hadn't complained about his social skills before.

"Well, it explains a lot," I finally said. "No turning potion. No peace between vampires and humans."

Liam shifted, crossing his arms over his chest as he leaned against the doorframe. "I learned something of interest today. The fae are having a meeting soon," he said after a pause. "To discuss the vampire attacks. The tension is getting worse, and from what I've heard, the fae might be preparing for more drastic measures."

I sat up straighter, my heart racing. "Like what?"

"An all-out war against your kind," he said quietly, almost reluctantly. "The fae don't take kindly to being threatened, especially by the Aislean. Your kin aren't coming to heel."

"Not my kin," I muttered under my breath, unwilling to claim those vampires and their reckless aggression. "It will all be fixed though," I tell him. "Soon."

He nodded slowly, like he doesn't believe me. "We can only hope it doesn't get worse before it gets better."

I again cursed myself for not paying closer attention during Clara's lessons on diplomacy and politics. But then an idea struck me like lightning. I stood abruptly, knocking the journal to the ground.

"I want to go," I said, surprising myself with the force behind my words.

Diary, though my first suggestion was without thought, it makes sense! If they're having a meeting to address vampire aggression, perhaps there is a way I can use the fae magic to find a path home. And if I'm lucky, maybe they'll even help me figure out why I was sent here in the first place. In exchange, I can confirm the aggression will end, and give them a bit of hope.

Of course, there is always the chance they'll kill me on the spot for meddling, but I'm not in the mood to dwell on that particular detail.

Now, when I'd suggested it to Liam, he didn't seem to understand my request, at first. "Go? To the fae meeting?"

"Yes," I said firmly. "If there's even a chance that the fae's magic could help me get back to my time, I need to be there. And besides..." I trailed off, a sly smile tugging at my lips. "It would certainly impress Clara to have a firsthand account of a fae meeting."

Liam stared at me, his expression unreadable. For a long moment, I wasn't sure if he was going to argue or outright refuse. But then, something shifted in his eyes.

He sighed, rubbing the back of his neck as if he was already regretting his decision. "You're going to get us both killed, you know that, right?"

"Come on," I teased, nudging his arm with my elbow. "It'll be fun. You might even enjoy yourself."

Liam shot me a look that said he doubted that very much, but there was a glint of something else there too—a sense of ease that hadn't been there before.

Maybe it's because he's slowly warming up to me, or maybe he has just resigned himself to me. Either way, it's a start.

Pity it will end soon, once the fae send me home.

Emma's Diary Entry

13th Day of the Harvest Moon, 1695

Dear Diary,

We leave at dawn.

The last few days have felt strangely peaceful, though I suspect that feeling won't last long. Liam and I have spent more time together than ever, and it wasn't intentional—just a natural consequence of preparing for the fae meeting.

Despite his usual prickly demeanor, I started to notice a softness in Liam that I haven't seen before. He was still moody, certainly, with his brooding silences and sharp remarks whenever I said something that rubbed him the wrong way. But it wasn't as hostile as it had been in the beginning. His sarcasm has shifted, become more playful, as if he's testing boundaries rather than trying to keep me at arm's length. And sometimes, when he doesn't think I'm looking, I catch him smiling—a small, fleeting curve of his lips that he tries to hide by turning away.

He even helped me understand some of the basic concepts of magical potions and spells yesterday, his voice patient as he explained the intricacies of the ingredients we needed to make the last set of tinctures to sell before we go.

"No, no, you're stirring too fast," he said, moving behind me, his hands briefly covering mine on the ladle. His touch sent a shock through me, a warmth that spread from where his fingers brushed mine. I could feel his breath against my ear, low and steady. "Like this. You need to coax it gently, or it'll curdle."

"Oh, so now you're an expert on coaxing?" I teased, tilting my head to look at him.

He didn't pull away. Instead, he smirked, his dark eyes glinting with mischief. "Maybe I am. I've had plenty of practice with you."

I couldn't help but laugh, the sound surprising me with its ease, like this—whatever this is between us—was something I could get used to.

Today, as we gathered supplies for the journey, I tested the waters a little more. "You could use some sun, you know. All that pale skin… If we get caught in a snowstorm on the trip, I'll lose you."

To my surprise, instead of snapping back with his usual dry retort, he glanced at me with a smirk, the corners of his eyes crinkling slightly. "I've heard worse," he said. "Besides, you're one to talk. You practically glow in the dark."

"I'll have you know my complexion has been described as a beautiful burnished gold," I retorted.

"Only by someone who is color blind," he replied with a roll of his eyes.

"Oh, please," I said, crossing my arms with mock severity. "I'm a vision of radiance."

Liam shook his head, but I saw the faintest trace of a smile tugging at his lips. "A vision of something," he muttered, gesturing toward the path back to his house.

The sun was dipping low, the last light filtering through the trees in soft, dappled patterns. It felt... peaceful. Almost normal. Like something I wanted to get used to.

And when we got back inside, we gathered the last of our things in relative silence, the only sounds the crackle of the fire and the rustle of papers and glass. I was lost in thought, running through all the potential outcomes from the meeting, wondering if the fae would take me home, when his gaze fell upon me.

His gaze was different this time—less guarded, more contemplative. He said nothing, just stood there for a moment, eyes lingering on me as though searching for something beneath the surface. Then, as if making some silent decision, he nodded once, a brief, almost imperceptible gesture.

He finished storing his ingredients and joined me in one of the chairs by the fire.

"You seem lost in thought." His eyes met mine, dark pools reflecting the remnants of the day.

So do you, I thought but didn't say. "Simply thinking about the meeting," I replied. "And what comes next." I had told him weeks ago about the treaty and the possibility of a turning potion.

"It seems unimaginable," he mused, gazing into the flames. "That there could be another option besides death. That some would actually choose it."

"Enough people do," I replied, thinking of the long lists of humans willing to be Turned.

His features grew somber, his eyes darkening with thought. "It's a stark choice, turning away from mortality. To lose one's humanity in exchange for eternal existence... to risk eternity alone. It is a curse disguised as a gift." He shook his head, the long strands of his hair hiding his face. "I don't know who would risk that."

I scooted closer to him, the space between us like a heavy, invisible wall. "You've been on your own for a long time, haven't you?" I asked, my voice softer than I intended.

Liam didn't answer at first. For a moment, I braced myself for his sharp retort, for the familiar edge to his words that came each time I pried. But instead, he sighed, a deep, weary sound that seemed to come from somewhere deep within him.

"Yes," he finally admitted. "I have."

There was a vulnerability in his voice I hadn't heard before, a crack in the armor he always wore. I watched him carefully, sensing there was more he wasn't saying, but I didn't want to push too hard. Instead, I offered a small smile. "Well, at least you're not alone anymore. For now, anyway."

His gaze met mine, softer than I'd ever seen it. "For now," he echoed, his voice almost gentle.

Then, as if to shake off the moment, he stood up and stretched, his usual cool demeanor sliding back into place. "Get some rest," he said, his voice gruff again. "We've got a long journey ahead."

And just like that, the weight of our conversation dissipated into the warmth of the crackling fire.

I'm not sure what tomorrow holds, but at least, for now, we're facing it together. For now, that's enough.

Journal Entry of Liam Matthews

14th day of the Harvest Moon, 1695

She sleeps now, finally—after hours of restlessness, rolling from one side to the other, her breaths uneven as though she fights a battle even in her dreams. I am grateful for the silence, if only for a few hours. The candle flickers beside me, casting dim shadows across the walls of this cramped, poorly ventilated room that we are forced to share.

Her presence lingers even when she is still. It's strange. I've grown so accustomed to being alone that the simple act of cohabitating with another person, especially one like her, seems foreign—unnerving even.

Yet, there's something about it that isn't entirely... unpleasant.

The journey to the fae's meeting has been grueling. The weather, true to form for this time of year, offered nothing but icy rain, leaving the roads a mess of mud and misery. She, of course, remained her usual infuriatingly optimistic self, remarking on the beauty of the landscape as though the world wasn't entirely falling apart around us. I said nothing. What is there to say? The trees, half-dead and skeletal, loomed like specters in the mist, and the rivers have swollen beyond their banks, threatening to swallow the roads whole. Nothing about this journey is beautiful.

Emma walked ahead, as she usually attempts to do, with an energy I envy. Her confidence is unsettling, as if the dangers we walk into are nothing more than a minor inconvenience. Perhaps that's a consequence of living in a future where peace is a given, where the unknown is less feared.

The worst part, though, is not the journey itself but the constant closeness. Sharing a home was...

tolerable. I had my space, she had hers. No matter that sometimes my space became hers. But on this trip, we've been forced into proximity that neither of us could have predicted or prepared for.

It was Emma's fault, naturally. Though she had no complaints about the muddy mess we slogged through, she demanded a bed indoors when it came time to sleep. Never mind that we were in the heart of the forest. She seemed to think that we'd stumble across a perfectly good inn simply because she desired it. Never mind that we'd seen no signs of civilization since midday.

But, through sheer luck or some force beyond explanation, we found one before the moon reached its zenith. The innkeeper didn't seem particularly bothered by our arrival, though his eyebrow did twitch ever so slightly when I requested a single room. Our flimsy lie of being newlyweds passed muster—barely. Emma, of course, found the whole situation terribly amusing.

"Married?" she'd teased, raising an eyebrow in that insufferable way she does. "I had no idea you were so eager to make an honest woman of me."

If I weren't so exhausted, I might've had a clever retort ready. Instead, I muttered something about tradition and customs and promptly made a fool of myself by blushing like a schoolboy when we saw the room.

Emma, true to form, seemed entirely unbothered. She tossed her bag onto the bed with all the nonchalance of someone used to far grander accommodations. I, on the other hand, couldn't stop fidgeting. She teased me about it, of course. But there was something gentler in her tone tonight, something that made it easier to bear.

"It's just sleep," she said, resting her hand on my arm for a moment. "Nothing more."

She's right, of course. It's just sleep. But I took the floor, naturally, though she insisted it wasn't necessary. I wouldn't, couldn't, have it any other way.

Still, as the hours crept by and her breathing grew steady, I couldn't help but notice how small she looked in that oversized bed. How vulnerable. It's odd to think of her in such terms. She carries herself with such a strange mix of strength and lightheartedness that it's easy to forget she's out of her element—thrust into a time that is not her own, surrounded by dangers she can't fully comprehend.

There were moments on the journey when I caught her glancing at me out of the corner of her eye, her expression unreadable. I don't know what she's looking for, and I haven't the patience to ask. But there is a growing sense between us—a quiet understanding, perhaps. We bicker, of course. We're far too different not to. But there's a rhythm now, one that is becoming familiar. I don't know if that should be comforting or alarming.

Journal of Liam Matthews

15th day of the Harvest Moon, 1695

WE BREACHED THE PORTAL today. I don't know what I was expecting, but it certainly wasn't this. It's... more than I can describe. The air hummed with magic—real magic, the kind that sends shivers down your spine even though you can't quite explain why.

The portal itself was remarkable, a shimmering gateway inside a dark cave that looked like it was made of light and water, though when I reached out, I felt nothing but a gentle warmth. I have never seen anything like it. I'm not sure I ever will again.

Emma, of course, was eager to plunge in, her eyes sparkling with reckless excitement I wish I could have shared. Apparently she traveled to Avalaruin often in her ~~old~~ regular life. But this—this was different. This wasn't some silly adventure. It was a doorway to another realm during times of strife, a world we know so little about, one that could very well swallow me whole.

She smiled at me when I hesitated, that playful, knowing smile that makes it impossible to stay rooted in my fear. "Shall we?" she asked, her voice so light, so full of promise.

But the world we were met with looked to be made in my image, rather than hers. I can't say I was surprised by the bleakness of the fae realm. Only fools expect beauty where ancient magics linger. Only fools expect joy when faced with something new. And I am no fool. Yet even my own experiences did not prepare me for the grotesque display of menace that greeted us.

The air shifted subtly at first—an insidious cold seeping into my skin. It wasn't physical discomfort alone but an unwelcome reminder that we'd trespassed into hostile territory. The light dimmed to a sickly hue, and shadows swallowed the sky. The atmosphere pressed in on us, as though the very air resented our presence.

The forest we entered was something out of my darkest nightmares—blackened trees twisted upward as if clawing for escape. Their branches loomed above, tangled and oppressive, blotting out the weak remnants of light. The ground squelched beneath our feet with an unnatural softness that made every step feel treacherous. Each movement threatened to pull us into the earth below, where who knows what horrors lay in wait. It was as if the forest itself were alive, not merely existing but *watching*—waiting, even.

Silence ruled here, not the comforting kind, but an absence of sound so complete it turned maddening. My ears strained for any sign of life, of movement, but there was nothing—no wind, no rustle of leaves, no birdsong. Nothing except the echo of my own heartbeat, which, I loathe to acknowledge even in this journal, had quickened.

We pressed on, though with every step deeper into the woods, the dread mounted. The path we followed narrowed, the trees growing closer together until we were forced to maneuver through a tangled mess of brambles and vines. Thorned tendrils snaked out from the undergrowth, as if to test us, twitching ever so slightly when we passed too near. I do not believe they were simply plants. Such things rarely are in a place like this.

When we reached the bridge to the mainland, it felt like a final warning. The structure was ancient—rickety at best, suicidal at worst. It spanned a chasm so deep, the bottom was lost to darkness, and the creaking ropes and cracked wooden planks did little to inspire confidence. Even now, the memory of that rickety deathtrap makes my stomach twist.

Of course, *she* didn't hesitate. Emma, with her endless bravado, strode forward as if the very fae were watching over her. Perhaps they were. I lingered for a moment, eyeing the boards with their gaps large enough to swallow a foot—possibly an entire person—before following. There was no other option, after all. The ropes groaned in protest under my weight, and the bridge swayed alarmingly in the wind. Every step brought with it the risk of a fatal plunge. But we crossed.

The mainland was no less foreboding. The twisted trees eventually gave way to a barren plain, cracked and lifeless underfoot. A single sign post appeared, directing us towards the fae council. And we pressed on.

Emma, of course, remained unfazed, her insufferable optimism undimmed by the surroundings. She seemed to find amusement in the most grotesque of places, as though we were simply on a grand excursion rather than walking into the lion's den.

I spent most of the remaining journey distracted by thoughts of the upcoming meeting. The fae are unpredictable at the best of times, and this meeting will not be one of those times. The tension in the air is thick. There is talk of war—whispers that grow louder with each passing day. And then there's her—this anomaly in time, this creature from another era who believes she can somehow stop the impending disaster. Her confidence is... misplaced, at best. Yet, there is a small part of me—a part I despise—that almost hopes she's right. Not that I'll tell her that.

I've tried to warn her, tried to tell her what she might be walking into. The fae have no love for vampires, especially not now. But she won't listen, of course. She's determined to go, determined to meddle. And for some reason, I've agreed to help her. I wonder if I'm a fool for doing so.

After hours of traversing that wretched, lifeless landscape, just when Emma began grumbling about needing to find another indoor bed, we came upon something so absurd it was nearly laughable: an inn. In the midst of this desolate fae realm, as though planted by Emma herself. The sight of it was such a stark contrast to our surroundings that I questioned for a moment whether we had stepped through yet another portal.

Its exterior was mismatched—a patchwork of wood, stone, and materials that shouldn't have held together under any natural laws. The roof sagged in the middle, covered in what appeared to be moss, though it glimmered faintly in the dim light, as though sprinkled with some manner of dust. Its windows were an odd assortment of sizes and shapes, some round, some square, and some entirely nonsensical, each one glowing with an eerie light that didn't seem to come from any normal source.

As we approached, the door creaked open of its own accord—a most *welcoming* gesture, no doubt. I was less than enthused. Emma, of course, strode inside without hesitation, seemingly unfazed by the peculiarities of our new surroundings. I followed, every sense on alert for trickery.

At the far end of the room, a figure stood behind what appeared to be a bar, though it was difficult to tell if it was wood or stone—or something in between. The figure itself was tall and thin, almost skeletal, dressed in clothing that seemed to flicker between outdated fashion and something wholly unfamiliar. Perhaps something from Emma's time. Its face was shrouded in shadow, its eyes the only clear feature—two glowing orbs that watched us with an unsettling intensity. It said nothing, only inclined its head slightly in what I assume was a gesture of acknowledgment.

"Charming," I muttered under my breath, though Emma appeared unfazed, offering the figure a polite nod before turning to me with that insufferable grin of hers.

"See? I told you we'd find somewhere to rest."

"Rest" hardly seemed appropriate for this place. Every inch of the inn felt alive, watching, waiting. There were no other guests as far as I could see, though the unsettling notion that we were not alone persisted. It was as though the inn itself was... sentient, observing us with as much curiosity as I observed it.

Our room was no better. The door led into a small, dimly lit space that was somehow both too warm and too cold at the same time. The bed—a monstrosity of a thing, cobbled together from what appeared to be bones and vines—seemed to pulse faintly, as if breathing. The walls were draped in thick, dark fabric that shifted subtly, as though alive with its own malevolent energy.

Emma, ever the optimist, flopped onto the bed with a contented sigh, as if we hadn't just walked into the embodiment of every bad dream imaginable. How she manages to find comfort in such a place is beyond me.

But she has. And she stirred earlier, mumbling something in her sleep. I didn't catch the words, but I think I heard my name.

I don't know why that unsettles me. It's not like we haven't been forced into each other's company long enough for her to start dreaming of me, though I can't imagine what sort of role I play in her subconscious.

Still, watching her now, I realize how much has changed since she first appeared in my life. I hadn't expected this—this strange camaraderie, a truce born out of necessity but growing into something more complex. I won't call it friendship. That would be too generous a term. But there is... something.

I'll keep my guard up, of course. Tomorrow will be a test—a test of my patience, of her resolve, and of whatever tenuous connection we've built during these past weeks. The fae will not be kind.

They never are. If she truly believes she can stand against them, I wish her luck. She'll need it.

The fire is dying now. But I must remain alert. If we make it through the night without being devoured by whatever lurks within these walls, it will be nothing short of a miracle.

Tomorrow, we face the fae. Tomorrow, we might face war. Tomorrow, she might learn that not every story ends the way she hopes.

Minutes of the Fae Elder Council Meeting

Half Day of Harvest Moonfall, 95th Year of Bearach

I. Call to Order The meeting was called to order at high noon by High King Bearach. The seven members of the Elder Council, all lords and ladies of the ancient fae lineages, took their seats. The High King opened the session with a declaration of purpose: to determine the fate of the vampires whose unchecked aggression had sparked turmoil across the realm.

II. Roll Call Present were:

- **High King Bearach** (Chairman)

- **Elder Fintan** of the Fiacha Lineage (Council Elder)

- **Elder Carlin** of the Gloine Grove (Council Elder), accompanied by Lady Veshra

- **Elder Braoin** of the Obsidian Hills (Council Elder)

- **Elder Guaire** of the Fáithmire Wood (Council Elder), accompanied by Lady Ilmarra

- **Elder Muireann** of the Cainneach Peaks (Council Elder), accompanied by Lord Dubh

- **Elder Nuala** of the Aithche Vale (Council Elder), accompanied by Lord Nuada

- **Elder Brid** of the Blaith Pass (Council Elder)

In attendance as well were heirs of the various fae lords and ladies, along with:

- **Governor Alistair Harrington**, representative of the human world, accompanied by Annabelle Harrington.

- A small delegation of vampire ambassadors, led by **Duchess Lidia**, leader of the pacifist covens seeking peace, accompanied by Duke Varian.

III. Reading of Grievances

The Elders each presented reports on the escalating conflict between the vampires and the non-magical races in the Aboveground. Reports of villages destroyed, forests ravaged, and human lives lost were read with great severity. Several audience members expressed concerns over the increasing threat posed by these rogue vampires, citing numerous casualties and the destruction of vital human territories, particularly those necessary for trade with Avalaruin.

It was noted that the rise in attacks was unprecedented in scale and intensity. The vampire delegation, solemn and subdued, was unable to counter the grievous charges brought against their kind.

Governor Harrington took the floor and presented a proposal to consider the eradication of the vampires if no solution to their unchecked aggression could be found. He acknowledged that this was an extreme measure but stressed that the survival of the fae and human realms depended on swift and decisive action. "The vampires have proven themselves a blight on this world," he declared. "It is time to consider their extermination for the safety of all other races. They are beyond saving."

IV. The Vote

A vote was requested, led by Elder Fintan. "If there is no cure for this aggression," he stated, "then there can be no place for vampires in this world." After a short recess, roll call was had and votes tallied:

- **Elder Fintan** in favor

- **Elder Carlin** in favor

- **Elder Braoin** in favor

- **Elder Guaire** against

- **Elder Muireann** against

- **Elder Nuala** in favor

- **Elder Brid** in favor

The vote passed, five in favor, two against.

V. Proposals for Eradication

Discussions shifted to potential strategies for the eradication of vampires. Plans were presented for a coordinated assault on vampire enclaves, utilizing fae magic to burn out their strongholds and minimize their deadly influence. Some Elders favored a gradual culling, others an outright extermination, as Governor Harrington continued to push for decisive action.

[pen scratches across the page]

VI. Disruption

A scuffle has just occurred. Two audience members, now confirmed to be uninvited, demanded to present before the Council.

Emma, a vampire unknown by Duchess Lidia or her company, and a human healer of no significant standing.

"What about the potion? What about the turned?" she demanded most outrageously.

High King Bearach, in his wisdom and patience, requested she speak. With reluctance at first, she proposed that the council consider the possibility of developing a new form of magic or potion to replicate or restore the control over the vampire's taking of human blood. She presented a most shocking plan: a potion drunk by humans, to protect them from death by the vampire's teeth. Instead, they are turned into a vampire themselves.

A discussion was had. The vampire delegation looked on with renewed hope, while the fae nobles in favor of eradication exchanged doubtful glances. The High King asked Emma if she would take on the responsibility of developing this method, and if she believed she could complete it in time to prevent further conflict. Emma agreed, but requested that a skilled mage be assigned to assist her. She named her companion as her desired partner in this endeavor.

The council deliberated, but no decision appeared to be made. No vote was tallied. Finally, High King Bearach spoke again, utilizing his royal decree to overturn the vote of the Council for the first time since the Cainneach Peaks debacle of 1040. "If there is even a chance that this solution could save lives, then we must pursue it. Emma, you and your companion are tasked with creating this potion."

VII. Conclusion

The meeting concluded with the Council agreeing to grant Emma and the healer the resources necessary to pursue the creation of this cure. While skepticism remained, the fae Elders allowed one last reprieve for the vampire race, contingent on the success of Emma's endeavor.

Emma and the healer are to report back to the council regularly on their progress. Duchess Lidia is to take the time provided to her to reach an agreement with the rogue covens to join the vampire's consulate.

VIII. Adjournment

The Council will reconvene in six moons to hear a progress report from both Emma and Duchess Lidia.

Recorded by Lady Ina Maoltuile, Scribe of the Council

Emma's Diary Entry

20th day of the Harvest Moon, 1695

Dear Diary,

We're back at Liam's farmhouse.

I don't know why my hands are still shaking as I write this. Maybe it's because of what I've done—or perhaps what I've set in motion. Maybe it's because of how furious Liam is, and how afraid I am that I've just lost my only ally. But I had no choice—it's true, isn't it? The Oracle confirmed

I'd be here, and travel this path. And the letter forced me here. I did what I had to.

I hope.

The meeting was two days ago, and we snuck in. We'd spent the night at a charming little inn run by a lesser fae creature who was incredibly polite (I've half a mind to introduce him to Clara once I return home). They didn't even ask for money, just kissed my palm when we checked-in and told me to sleep well! But Liam ushered us out before dawn. He claimed it was to get ahead of the others, but I think it was mostly to keep himself busy—nerves, perhaps.

Getting there early didn't help. The session was closed to outsiders—only fae heirs and the official retinues from the human and vampire contingents were permitted inside. The guards' silver eyes watched the doors with unblinking vigilance. But with some careful maneuvering, we slipped in, posing as invited guests. I tried to catch sight of the vampire contingent, hoping to recognize someone, anyone. Duchess Lidia's name floated up from some dusty corner of my memory, a cadet branch of the family. That neither the King nor Queen attended should have been a relief, that the risk of this meeting wasn't high.

But no. This was an important meeting, perhaps the most important in the history of my kind. The air in that room was thick with tension—anger barely concealed under the veneer of politeness.

And then the High King spoke. "Unless vampires can curb their innate aggression, we shall have no choice but to eradicate them." His voice cut through the room like frost settling on a clear night. One by one, the elders spoke, each ready to vote vampires into oblivion. I could see it in their faces—Elder Fintan, Elder Carlin, Elder Braoin—stern, unyielding.

My heart pounded, thudding in my chest as I waited for someone—anyone—to speak up. Someone had to appear, someone had to propose the turning potion. The time was right. Only a few more years and the first Turned would be made, leading to a magical treaty between the vampires and humans. Then all talk of eradication would be moot.

But no one spoke. And then they debated their plans—how to root out the vampire enclaves, how to destroy us—but still I waited. I waited for someone to mention the potion. Someone had to know about it. My stomach twisted in knots as the minutes went on.

And then, it struck me. All my plans for this meeting—finding a way home, discovering why I was here—all vanished, leaving my thoughts like wisps of smoke. The threads of time were a tangled weave, said the Oracle, but in that moment, they unraveled to reveal a path so clear I wondered how I could've ever missed it. I was the one who knew about the potion, the only one who understood what it could do. I had the knowledge, and if no one else would bring it up, I would. This whole time, I thought I was a victim of fate, but I was part of the story all along.

Before I knew what I was doing, I was on my feet, pushing past people, elbows and shoulders jostling against me as I stumbled towards the front of the room. It's as though I was drugged, Diary, because in what other world would I willingly volunteer for extra duties? I vaguely recall knocking someone over, but all I could focus on was stopping the discussion from continuing. One of the fae guards moved toward me as if to drag me away, but I didn't give him a chance.

"Wait!" I shouted. My voice felt too loud, too shaky for a place like this, but it cut through the noise. The room fell silent, all eyes turning to me. An uninvited guest, an intruder in a council that had already decided my fate. The weight of their disdain settled over me, but I pressed on.

"You can't do this," I said. "What about the potion?"

The fae elders exchanged wary glances, and the room buzzed with murmurs of confusion.

"Potion?" Elder Fintan sneered, his lips curling back like a wolf baring its teeth. "And what would you, an outsider, know of such things?"

I swallowed my nerves and stood taller, the princess that I was, willing to account for it for once (although I hope it doesn't become a habit). "I know that there's a way to stop the aggression," I said. "Vampire feeding mustn't be a death sentence. It can be controlled. Peace will come from it." Gone was the girl who shied away from responsibility, replaced by a woman fueled by the fire of possibility. "The potion—*I can create it.*" The words spilled from my lips, sounding absurd, but they were true. The threads of fate had pulled me here for this very reason.

For a heartbeat, the room was utterly still. The High King's gaze narrowed. "And you truly believe this can be done?" he asked, his tone edged with skepticism.

"Yes." The word came out stronger than I expected. "But I'll need help."

And that's when I made my next move. I turned to find Liam. He was standing at the back, trying his hardest to blend into the shadows. I didn't give him the chance. "I have a healer who can help me," I said, motioning toward him.

For a moment, I saw a flicker of something in his eyes—shock, maybe even anger. I hadn't asked for his permission. I hadn't even warned him. I simply threw him into the fray with me, expecting him to step forward. And he did, a better friend to me than I was to him, it seems, Diary.

The council deliberated in low, uncertain murmurs. I stood there, waiting for their decision, tapping my foot against the marble floor, counting the seconds that stretched on. They weren't convinced. But they would agree. History said they would.

Finally, the High King spoke, his voice heavy with finality. "You will create this potion," he decreed. "And you will return in six months."

Six months. Another six months trapped in this time. But I suppose it was always meant to be.

The journey to the farmhouse was tense. Liam barely spoke. I could feel the fury radiating off him. We walked in silence, the gloomy woods a mirror of the mood between us. The sun had long since dipped below the horizon, leaving us in darkness as we traveled back to the creaking wooden bridge that led to the portal, over the black waters of the Unseen Lake.

We could have stopped for the evening. On the way to the meeting, I'd demanded it the second the sun set. But the irritation rolling off Liam had me quicken my pace and agree to walk through the night.

After we breached the portal, once we were back in the Aboveground, he stopped. "Why?" he demanded, turning to face me, his eyes blazing with anger. "Why would you drag me into this?"

I blinked, taken aback. "I thought you'd want to help."

"Help?" His voice was sharp, slicing through the darkness. "You didn't even ask me, Emma. You just threw me in front of the council."

"I—" I opened my mouth to respond but faltered. I simply knew that he had to be the one to help me, Diary. He had the skills, the knowledge. If I was the vampire to set the potion in motion, he was the mage whose name was lost to time.

All I could manage was, "I'm sorry." It felt inadequate. Hollow. But it was all I had.

Liam didn't respond. He simply turned away, jaw clenched, and we continued in silence.

I just hope I haven't ruined everything.

Emma's Diary Entry

17th Day of the Hunter's Moon, 1695

Dear Diary,

It's been just more than a month since the council meeting, but the weight of that day still presses down on me like a heavy cloak I can't shrug off. I'm sure now that some magic guided my steps that day because if I'd truly had my wits about me, I never would have chosen this: to stand here at Liam's farmhouse, struggling to create a potion that seems beyond reach, tethered to a man who resents me with every breath.

Liam... he's been so quiet. His frustration has become a constant presence, like a storm cloud hanging over us, rumbling with thunder I can't quite hear but feel in every step he takes. It's become its own kind of torture. Not that he was ever particularly talkative, but before, there was a softness to his silence, a quiet companionship in those first few weeks after I'd arrived.

I thought, perhaps, time would heal this rift, that once he'd had space to process everything, he'd come around. Like he had come around to me when I'd first arrived. But nothing has changed since the meeting. It's made my volunteerism unbearable.

I'm unused to people angry with me. I'm the amusing one, the princess always game for a romp, charming her way out of trouble with a grin. Even at her most frustrated, Clara would just shake her head at my antics, as if to say, "That Emma." Because that's who I am. But this time, my recklessness has come back to bite me.

I kept replaying the moment I volunteered him in my head. It seemed so clear at the time, like fate had led me there, and the only thing to do was step forward. Now I see it through his eyes. I didn't ask. I didn't consider his feelings or his past. I was so caught up in the significance of my role, in fulfilling what I believed was destiny, why I'd been brought through time, that I dragged him along with me. But I never expected him to be so... angry at me. I never expected to feel this helpless.

It wasn't until last night, sitting by the fire after another long day of research, that he finally said something that made me understand. He didn't say it directly—he never does—but, he let it slip. I knew there was pain in his past, something dark and unresolved that he kept locked away, only offering glimpses of it when his defenses were down. He never speaks of his family, or why he's the outcast of the town, but I've seen the haunted look in his eyes when memories slip through.

But he spoke about choices. He said, in that low voice of his, almost like he was talking to the flames instead of me, that for most of his life, he had no say in his own fate. Only when he became an adult did he finally begin to carve his own path. His parents had wanted him to be a soldier, and after they died, the town pushed him even harder, demanding he avenge their deaths, to pick up the sword and become a warrior. But he couldn't. Not when he had my letter in his pocket—a message from his future self.

"How could I become a vampire killer," he murmured, his voice barely more than a whisper, "when my future self told me I welcomed one into my home?"

So instead, he spent years trying to appease the townsfolk in other ways, learning magic to placate their expectations. Not quite the soldier they wanted, but maybe a warmage could be enough. And still, that letter remained, a quiet rebellion in his pocket. When the time came for him to join a coven and fulfill their expectations, he refused. He chose to be a healer, using his skills to help rather than harm. The town saw it as a betrayal, an abandonment of his duty. They wrote him off as a failure, a disappointment, never forgiving him for not becoming the hero they wanted him to be.

And then, in the council chamber, I did the same thing. Without even realizing it, I placed him on another path he didn't choose. I told the world he was only worthy if he did what I wanted, what *we* needed. And now, I can see why he's been so angry. It's not just about me, or the situation. It's about the years he spent carrying burdens that were never his to bear. And I've added to them, for however long I'm meant to stay.

But how do I fix this? What's done is done—the fae have already tasked us with this monumental responsibility, and there are no take-backs. I need him. The world needs him. But how do I ask him to keep walking this path when I'm the one who set it before him without a second thought?

I wouldn't, if I were in his place. I didn't, back home. I know the feeling all too well—the constant battle with Clara, with Demara, with all the advisors who tried to mold me into something I wasn't. I wanted to do what I wanted, not what someone else demanded.

What I do know is this: I won't let this responsibility crush him. I won't be another weight around his neck. We'll find a way through this together, even if it means I have to carry more of the burden myself.

Is this what Demara feels like all the time? This merciless weight of responsibility, this constant, gnawing dread?

It's awful. I hate it. I hate—

I hate that I hurt him.

Note left by Liam for Emma

I am astounded by your ability to remain upbeat in the face of potentially disastrous potion failures. It is truly a marvel—much like watching a phoenix try to swim.

Also, please confine your irrepressible optimism to non-critical moments; the potion is not improved by your relentless mirth.

And no, the potion will not benefit from your 'lively dance routine' to encourage its reaction.

Note left by Emma for Liam

I promise to keep the dancing to a minimum during critical moments. Perhaps I'll save it for when we finally get the potion right—think of it as a celebratory dance of sorts.

The herbs you asked for are drying by the window. I made you tea as well—I figured you could use a break. Don't overwork yourself.

And... thank you again for all your help.

Note left by Liam for Emma

There is no need for a 'pep talk' on the importance of "positive energy" in the brewing process.

Thank you for the tea.

Emma's Diary Entry

18th day of the Ice Moon, 1696

Dear Diary,

It's been four months since the council, four months since I threw us onto this path. Funny how the world can change and stay exactly the same all at once. Somewhere in these months, the tension between Liam and me has eased, though I can't quite pinpoint when or why. There was no grand gesture, no teary-eyed apology to sweep everything away. It just... happened, like a bruise slowly fading.

I didn't ask for forgiveness, and I doubt he ever truly gave it. We just found a way to coexist. At first, the silence between us was thick, pressing, heavier than I was used to. I tried everything to shatter it—jokes that fell flat, attempts at small talk that hit walls, even bringing up ridiculous topics like the merits of boiled vegetables (spoiler: there are none). But somewhere along the line, that silence changed. Became... comfortable. Maybe we realized we're all each other has. No room for anger or resentment when you're the only two people in the world who understand what it's like to fail over and over again at something that feels so crucial.

And fail we have, Diary. The right blend of magic and herbs slips through our fingers every time, no matter how many combinations we try. Each new attempt seems destined for disappointment. I'm starting to wonder if we're just placeholders, waiting for the real vampire-mage duo to show themselves and take over, take away the responsibility.

But it remains bearable. Once all the resentment between us (on his side) settled, the notes came. It started small—Liam leaving a scrap of parchment on my desk, a reminder of some obscure detail in an old tome or a suggestion for an ingredient we hadn't yet dared to use. I replied with a note of my own, and soon enough, our scribblings turned from practical to... something else. A joke about my terrible penmanship, a wry comment about the stink of the latest concoction, a tiny bridge between us.

It's become our secret language, these little bits of paper left among our work. Sometimes, he'd scrawl a comment so darkly funny that it made me smile despite myself. Other times, I'd sketch a ridiculous caricature of him, hunched over his books with an impossibly furrowed brow. Once, I left a note in his favorite book, something about how a certain plant smelled worse than his boots, which led to a whole back-and-forth of ever-more-ridiculous insults, until we both ended up laughing. Liam, laughing, truly laughing! I hope I can etch that sound into my memory forever.

Not that we don't still argue. We're both stubborn as stones and too invested to give up easily. But the arguments are different now. Less sharp, less bitter. More like two people railing against the universe instead of at each other. And after every argument, there's always a moment where our eyes meet, a half-smile appears, and we silently say, "Well, that didn't work. What's next?"

But that's the question, isn't it? What's next? Liam won't tell me what was in that damn note, the one that supposedly says how long I have left here. "Not long," he keeps saying. But will I be here long enough to finish this? To see it through to the end? Or will I leave him to muddle through it alone, with only our scribbled notes for company, on the path I put him on?

Guilt is a terrible feeling.

Note left by Emma for Liam

I wrote you a poem today:

> Aconite is beauty supreme
> But all is not what it seems
> Though its petals seem sweet,
> Its danger discreet,
> Of poisons, it reigns as the queen

Finger's crossed the aconite infusion works.

SPECIAL EDITION

✶ Laidir Daily ✶

VOL. 11, NO. 6 *16TH DAY OF THE MOURNING MOON* *ABYEAR 1695*

FAE COUNCIL FOUL-UP

In a surprising twist, the High King, who had once advocated for the extermination of vampires, has notably shifted his stance. Reports suggest that the High King's previously staunch position against vampires has softened, leading to a reconsideration of his plans.

It is widely believed that this change of heart was influenced by private discussions with individuals knowledgeable about vampire lore.

Although the specifics of these discussions remain confidential, it is rumored that the High King's revised stance is connected to the development of a potion intended to facilitate the turning of vampires.

HUMAN-MADE VAMPIRES? OVER OUR DEAD BODIES. LITERALLY.

HUMAN TRAITOR?

Sources say a human mage attended the council meeting and is the driving force behind the so-called 'turning potion.' Little is known about this turncoat. One wonders if he has been insulated from the vampire threat...

CONTINUED ON PAGE 3

THE LAIDIR DAILY IS DELIGHTED TO ANNOUNCE THE UNION OF MISS ELIZA FAIRBROOK, RENOWNED HERBALIST AND FIRSTBORN OF THE ESTEEMED FAIRBROOK FAMILY, TO MR. GREGORY THORNWICK, ESTEEMED PRINTER AND SECOND SON OF THE LAIDIR THORNWICKS. DUE TO THEIR UPCOMING BRIDAL TOUR, ALL EDITIONS WILL BE ON HOLD UNTIL THE SECOND WEEK OF THE MOURNING MOON.

Emma's Diary Entry

10th day of the Pink Moon, 1696

Dear Diary,

I'm still here. Though that's probably a good thing, since we've made no significant progress on the potion. I know it must happen at some point. But when?

What was it Clara said on that last evening? The two hundredth anniversary of something for the Turned was coming. The anniversary of the first agreed-to turning? Of the creation of their lordship under us? Or of the potion? If the former, we could create the potion at any time. If the latter, it could be thirteen more years of me here.

We were summoned back to Avalaruin, and the sight of the city was a stark reminder of how much the world has changed since our last visit. The once-lovely inn where we stayed had been reduced to a heap of charred timbers, its roof caved in and walls blackened by fire. The streets felt emptier, like the city itself was holding its breath. But the King's impatience hadn't dimmed in the slightest. This time, it was just the three of us—no council members perched like a flock of judgmental ravens, their eyes boring into us from above. Liam walked beside me, his face tight, as if every step was leading him to the gallows.

"Cheer up," I whispered, nudging his arm as we walked down the long, echoing aisle toward the King's dais. "Maybe he's discovered a newfound appreciation for failure."

Liam shot me a look—a mix of irritation and that begrudging amusement that he seems to reserve only for me.

We stood before the King like children caught with broken pieces of a treasured heirloom. His eyes were as sharp as a honed blade, narrowing on us from his high throne. He looked tired, angry, maybe even desperate—frustrations I understand all too well. I'd hoped to be done by now, back in my world where electric lights flicker in the streets, where automobiles hum past, and restaurants serve food that isn't boiled into oblivion.

"I expected more progress," the King finally said, his voice like ice scraping against stone.

I felt a spark of defiance. "We're trying our best, Your Majesty. We are attempting to create something that has never been created."

Liam tightened his grip on our tattered notes. His knuckles were almost white, but his voice stayed steady. "Indeed, Your Majesty. The fusion of alchemy and magic is delicate and unprecedented. We're on the cusp of a breakthrough."

The King's face remained unreadable. Silence stretched through the chamber, thick and heavy, broken only by the distant crackle of torches. I held my breath, forcing myself to keep my chin high.

At last, the King spoke again, softer but no less commanding. "I understand the complexity, but time is not a luxury we possess. This endeavor may not be viable."

"It is," I cut in, my voice sharper than intended.

His eyes flicked over to me, weighing my words. "How much time do you need?" he asked.

I hesitated. Saying *between a day and thirteen years* is probably more flippant than I could get away with when not wearing my heir circlet from Aislean.

(And see, Diary, this is called *maturing*.)

"That...I don't know," I finally said.

His patience visibly thinned. "You make bold claims with no certainty to back them. Why should I continue to entertain this—this folly?"

"Because," I said, the words escaping before I could stop them, "I know it will work. I know it has to."

He raised an eyebrow, his voice dangerously low. "And how, pray tell, could you possibly know that?"

I hesitated. This was it—the moment I hadn't planned for, hadn't prepared. The silence stretched, Liam glancing at me, his brow furrowed with concern. I took a deep breath and squared my shoulders.

"Because I'm not from here. Not really," I blurted out. "I'm... from the future."

The King's eyes widened ever so slightly, and Liam let out a strangled noise beside me, somewhere between a cough and a gasp.

"Explain yourself," the King demanded.

"I know it sounds absurd," I rushed on, "but I come from a time centuries ahead. In that time, your line still reigns. You have a son, a successor. I... I can't prove it, not in any way that you could see tomorrow, but it's true. And that's why I know this potion is worth the effort. Because I know that it must work... that it does work."

The King's stare was piercing, searching my face for any sign of deceit. "You expect me to believe that you've traveled across time, that your knowledge is based on... the future?"

"Yes." My voice was steady, despite the hammering of my heart. Liam's eyes widened in horror beside me, but I kept going. "And the potion will work. It will stop the violence."

The King frowned. "You're sure of this?"

"I know it," I insisted, raising my chin. "And it happens around this time. I don't recall exactly when," I admitted, heat rising in my cheeks at the reminder of my inadequacy, "but it's soon. Unless," I added with a hint of hope, "someone else has stepped forward to take on this task, now that they've heard of it?"

His expression softened, almost... amused? "No," he replied slowly. "No one else has been foolish enough to try." Finally, he nodded. "Very well. So long as Governor Harrington doesn't re-petition this council, you may have the time you need. Keep my advisors apprised of your progress."

I thought that was the end of it. But the moment we stepped outside, Liam grabbed my arm, pulling me away from prying eyes.

"Are you out of your mind?" he hissed. "Do you have any idea what you've just done?"

I shrugged, trying to brush it off. "I gave him a reason to let us keep working. Wasn't that the point?"

He ran a hand through his long hair, frustration deepening the furrows on his forehead. "Emma, you don't understand. They could imprison you—hunt you down for—"

"—For what I know?" I interrupted with a grin. "Torture me for all the secret knowledge I'm supposed to have? Good luck to them. I barely remember my own history lessons." I laughed. "But if they're interested in the best places to dine in the mage settlement two centuries from now, I'm their girl."

He didn't laugh. Instead, he leaned in, his voice almost a growl. "This isn't a joke, Emma. You're risking everything on a whim. Someone could hurt you, or worse."

I pulled back, a flare of anger rising. "This is my choice, Liam. My risk to take. Not yours."

He let out a sharp breath, his eyes searching mine. "Why do you have to make everything so... difficult?"

"Because easy gets us nowhere," I shot back. "And if you had a better plan, then you could have said it."

For a moment, we just stared at each other, the tension hanging thick in the air. Then he shook his head, muttering something under his breath that I couldn't quite catch.

"Why are you so angry?" I asked, softer this time. "It wasn't about you. It's about getting the time we need. I thought you'd appreciate that."

"Maybe it's because I care what happens to you," he said, almost too quietly.

My breath caught in my throat, and I had no idea how to respond. He turned away before I could find the words, leaving me standing there, more confused than ever.

I don't know what I expected... but I didn't expect this.

Note left by Liam for Emma

Found an old text that might be helpful. It's on your bed. Don't stay up too late reading—sleep is important too, even for immortals We'll try belladonna tomorrow if you continue to insist.

Note left by Emma for Liam

You were right about the belladonna. I'm beginning to think you're better at this than I am. Shocking! Try not to gloat too much.

I wrote you another poem as a consolation:

> Belladona is no mortal's plant
> To ingest it, know that you can't
> Unless death is your aim
> With your insides inflamed
> And a fate that's decidedly scant

Note left by Liam for Emma

The rhyming dictionary I acquired seems to be useful already. Better than when you attempted to rhyme 'amaryllis' with 'judicious.'

Emma's Diary Entry

6th day of the Dispute Moon, 1696

Dear Diary,

A year, Diary. An entire year since that cursed council meeting where I promised miracles with a confidence I didn't quite have, and here we are—no closer to a solution than we were back then. No magic formula, no perfect blend of herbs, no miraculous combination to save the day. Just days melting into nights, ink staining every fingertip, cauldrons bubbling over, and a relentless pursuit that feels like it's consuming everything.

But today, something happened—something unexpected that broke through the fog of endless failure.

The day began like every other in Liam's lab, which, let's be honest, has taken over the entire downstairs of the farmhouse by now. With a flick of my wrist, I sent a cloud of crystalline powder spiraling into the cauldron, where it fizzled and popped in the simmering elixir.

"Liam," I called out without looking up, certain he'd be buried deep in one of his ancient texts. "What was that spell again? The one about the moon's shadow and blood's whisper?"

His voice came back to me immediately, clear and steady as always: "*'Neath Luna's veil, silent as the night, blood of kin must speak but slight.'*" He rattled it off as easily as breathing, like reciting poetry. His ability to memorize entire passages never ceases to astound me—and, if I'm honest, make me a little envious. Especially when they sound so beautiful. In his deep voice, it's downright addictive.

"Right," I mumbled, scribbling his words next to my own indecipherable notes. I swallowed down the shiver that ran through me, one that had nothing to do with the cold draft seeping through the cracked windows and everything to do with Liam.

"Emma, you've got a smudge," he pointed out, his gaze fixed on my cheek. It was probably the ash from the sage we burned earlier, which left the entire room smelling like a campfire that went a bit too wild.

"Occupational hazard," I replied, rubbing at my cheek, not really caring if I made it worse. Liam crossed the room, and before I could blink, his thumb brushed against my skin, wiping the ash away with a gentleness that made my breath catch. I turned back to the cauldron, pretending the heat in my cheeks was just from the fire.

"Let's try this again," I said, a little too loudly, reaching for the latest wolfsbane extract. I measured out the drops carefully. New infusion, new hope, or so I told myself. Beside me, Liam ground herbs in that methodical way of his, the soft rhythm filling the air like a heartbeat. Our shoulders nearly touched as we leaned over the cauldron, both of us focused. He didn't seem affected at all by the proximity. Only I was pretending I didn't notice how close we were.

As I let a bead of his blood fall into the brew, our fingers brushed—just for a moment—but long enough for a spark to run up my spine.

"Perfect drop," he murmured, his voice so low I almost felt it rather than heard it. A smile tugged at my lips despite myself.

There was something different in the way he'd been looking at me recently, but I'm not putting a name to it. No need to overcomplicate things here, not when I'm still due home. "Not long," he reminded me so often.

"Thanks," I whispered, trying not to dwell on how his hand seemed to linger near mine, his touch so subtle it could almost be an accident. But accidents never made my heart race like this.

"We should record the reaction time," I suggested, desperate for a distraction from the fluttering sensation in my chest. Liam nodded, his expression shifting back to focus, but I caught him stealing another glance as I scribbled down the time, his gaze tracing my face.

Then, unexpectedly, he handed me a small gift, a worn leather-bound book. "For the anniversary of your arrival," he explained, a shy smile playing on his lips. "You looked close to finishing the one you came with."

I flipped it open and found a pressed flower tucked between the pages—a hellebore, pale and fragile, its scent still faintly clinging to the petals. Hellebore only blooms in winter, meaning he must have plucked it and kept it, preserved it until he gave it to me. It was a simple gesture, but it felt like something deeper. I feel a bit foolish for how much it meant to me. He could surely tell, he's always reminding me how unsubtle I am. But I couldn't help the warmth spreading through my chest.

"The pages are spelled," he continued. "They will never run out."

I beamed at him. "I didn't get you anything," I confessed.

"Your relentless optimism is gift enough," he teased, and I laughed. It felt like breathing after holding my breath for too long.

"It's not a punishment anymore?" I asked, teasing him back.

"No," he said quietly, his brown eyes heavy with meaning. "Not anymore."

Being here isn't all that bad, Diary.

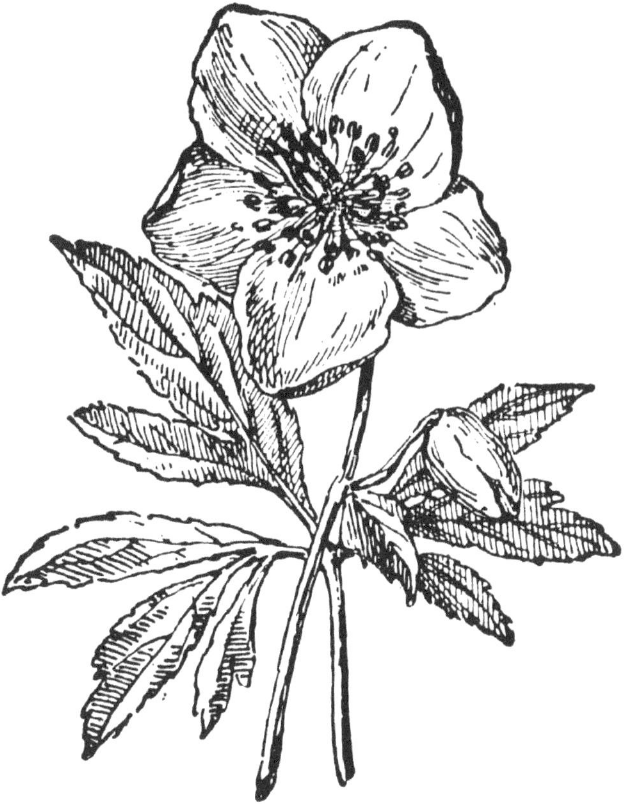

Note left by Liam for Emma

In shadowed glades where secrets keep
the hellebore child begins to creep.
A flower pale or petals dark
that begins its bloom in winter's arc.

Her beauty holds a poisoned sting,
a silent, deadly offering.
She bends not to the autumn's sun
but thrives when other blooms are done.

For those who seek her winter's bloom,

SHE WHO TURNS THE VAMPIRE

beware the whispers in the gloom.
For hellebore, with its quiet grace
is both a gift and grim embrace.

A healer's touch, a mage's bane,
she walks the line 'twixt loss and gain.
In gardens wild or cultivated,
her presence lingers, venerated.

Emma's Diary Entry

25th day of the Ice Moon, 1696

Dear Diary,

I found a poem tucked into my notebook today, nestled between my own scrawls and half-formed ideas. The handwriting was unmistakably his—sharp, precise, with a kind of order that seems to elude me. And the words...

He wrote about hellebore. Its contradictions, its beauty laced with danger. I've read nothing like it—each line felt like a secret, something fragile and real. I don't know what to make of it. I don't know if he meant it for me or if it was just a moment of his mind wandering across the page.

I still have the hellebore he gave me, its pale petals pressed between the pages of this journal. Now, that flower feels like more than just a gift. With the poem, it's as though I've acquired another piece of him, a delicate fragment of his mind and heart preserved between the pages...

Journal Entry of Liam Matthews

25th day of the Ice Moon, 1696

It's madness, truly.

The letter I wrote myself seemed fanciful, the words of a different man. There's no room for sentiment now, no time for... whatever it is that's growing between us. But I can't help it. I warned myself of this, but did nothing to stop it. She's brought something into my life I'd long buried—a flicker of connection, a feeling that I might belong somewhere again.

I've always been skilled with words that cut, words that can draw blood. But words that heal? Those aren't mine. Not like hers. But I'm trying, in my own way. I want her to see that I don't resent her for her presence or what she did, even if I cannot find a way to say it.

Note left by Emma for Liam

You didn't eat dinner again. I left some soup on the stove for you. Don't let it go cold like last time.

Emma's Diary Entry

28th day of the Dispute Moon, 1697

...and he was looking at me again. In that new way he has. I wanted to say something, anything, to cut through the strange tension building between us, to shatter it with some clever remark or witty comment. Instead, all I managed was a nervous, half-laugh.

"Liam, if we keep at this much longer, we'll both go mad," I said, trying to sound lighthearted, though my voice wavered slightly.

His smile was slow, almost teasing. "Maybe we already have," he said, but there was that softness to his voice, the one he seems to have so often now, a hint of something that felt like hope—or something more dangerous.

"Speak for yourself," I shot back, trying for lightness. "I was mad long before this started."

His laughter rang out, rich and warm, filling the confined space with its infectious sound. It's become my favorite sound, Diary.

And we stood there, caught between the unspoken things that had begun to stir in the spaces between our words, between our failures and our shared frustrations. And just for a moment, I wondered if we weren't searching for the wrong answer entirely. If maybe there was something else to be found here.

But I shook the thought away and forced a smile. "Well, mad or not, let's get back to it," I said, pretending my heart wasn't racing.

He nodded, but there was a look in his eyes that made me think he was wondering the same thing...

Note left by Liam for Emma

I noticed you've been working late. You're not the only one who can leave notes reminding others to rest. Consider this your reminder.

Emma's Diary Entry

10th day of the Harvest Moon, 1698

Dear Diary,

Another year gone by, and still no closer to the answer. I should be frustrated, panicked even, but... I'm not. Instead, there's this quiet contentment that's settled over me, a peace that comes from the rhythm we've fallen into, the routine we've built together.

I find myself wondering—what would my life look like if I stayed? It's a dangerous thought, one I shouldn't let myself entertain, but it's there all the same. I can't help it. There's something here, something between us, that I'm not quite ready to let go of.

I don't know how long this will last. He never tells me, never gives word to my time here. All I know is we likely have an expiration date of eleven years. *That blasted anniversary with details I still can't recall.*

Would I stay after? Once I've done what time and fate and magic have demanded?

~~Is there a way to change it?~~

I'm not ready to return.

Note left by Emma for Liam

I've been thinking about what you said last night. You're right, we need to focus more on the magical properties. Let's try that tomorrow.

(Your idea about the moon cycles was brilliant.)

Journal Entry of Liam Matthews

5th day of the Claiming Moon, 1700

I'VE STOPPED EXPECTING THE day she'll leave. Foolish, I know. I've learned better than to hope for things that don't last. But it's impossible to picture this place without her now. She's woven herself into my days and nights, into every corner of this house.

But I know the truth of it. I've told myself in that letter, as if to brace my heart. One day, she'll find the answer we've been chasing, and she'll go. And I'll still be here, left with a silence that will feel like a wound.

I don't know when it changed, when she became... everything. *The center of my world.*

I don't know how I'll bear it when she's gone.

Emma's Diary Entry

22nd day of the Quiet Moon, 1701

~~Must I return?~~

Note left by Emma for Liam

You looked tired today. I hope you're taking care of yourself. You *are* getting older. How long do humans live? Kidding.

The work can wait—your well-being can't.

Note left by Liam for Emma

Stop making that face, you know the one with your nose scrunched just so, when you're thinking too hard. You'll give yourself a headache.

Emma's Diary Entry

12th day of the Mead Moon, 1702

Dear Diary,

I've been thinking about happiness lately—what it truly means. I always thought it was found in a whirlwind, a life constantly in motion: nights filled with laughter, the thrill of a new dress, a stolen moment of mischief. But with Liam, I've discovered a different kind of happiness—quieter, deeper, one that doesn't demand or rush but simply asks me to be.

Liam and I have managed to carve out a life in the wilderness. A home. A routine. We've fought and argued, found comfort in each other's company, and learned to coexist even in the face of all the tension that hangs between us. He has grown grayer, more worn by the years than I ever thought possible for him. And I've found myself thinking more and more about how much I will miss the sound of his laughter, that unrestrained, joyful noise he only allows himself in rare moments.

I've grown here. Not just older, but into myself. The girl who once danced around her duties now stands firm, guiding our experiments with a certainty I never knew I possessed. ~~If~~ When I go back... Clara will hardly recognize me.

Note written by Liam

Torn and tossed in the trashcan

This morning's sunrise was particularly beautiful. It made me think of you. Perhaps you'll join me tomorrow?

Journal Entry of Liam Matthews

13th day of the Mourning Moon, 1703

THE YEARS HAVE GONE by like a breath, yet every moment with her stands clear in my mind. That sentimentality I believed would never build has overcome me, like a blazing fire, burning out everything but her.

She is everything now—a part of my life so constant I can't imagine a world without her. We've carved out something here, a life that speaks more in quiet moments and shared looks than in words.

I've fallen for her slowly, quietly—so quietly, I've never said it out loud. But I think she knows. There's a comfort in our silence, in the way we speak through small notes and simple gestures. It's a kind of love that doesn't ask for declarations, one that's grown deep and steady over time.

I wrote it to myself, a warning: *Because no matter how much you wish you could change the outcome, you cannot. Her path is set, as is yours. You'll need these memories when you spend the rest of your life alone.*

I want to tell her, to say the words, but fear keeps me quiet. I'm afraid of what speaking them might change, of losing what we have. I need these memories, I told myself this in permanent ink. Why would I risk them?

I'm running out of time.

SPECIAL EDITION
✶ LAIDIR DAILY ✶

VOL. 10, NO. 4   10TH DAY OF THE MOURNING MOON   ABYEAR 1704

HARRINGTON'S FAILURE

THIS MENACE WILL NOT END UNTIL WE END IT

Governor Harrington, where are you?

Your promises to protect the realm ring hollow while our people are hunted in the night!

Citizens, how much longer must we endure the growing shadow of the vampire scourge? Their bloodlust knows no bounds, their disdain for human life evident in every drained corpse left to rot in our streets!

It's time for action—not words. We demand curfews, armed patrols, and kill on sight orders for any vampire. Enough is enough. Either the governor acts, or the people will take matters into their own hands.

People, sharpen your stakes.

DRAGON SIGHTING?
OR GIANT BIRD?

A massive shadow and the sound of wings were seen and heard over the northern highlands last week. Local shepherds claim a dragon has returned to the region, though skeptics dismiss it as a particularly large bird...

CONTINUED ON PAGE 4

Emma's Diary Entry

31st day of the Claiming Moon, 1705

Dear Diary,

It happened. Even now, I can scarcely believe it, hours later, my heart still thundering, my lips still warm.

After so many failed attempts—so many long days, longer nights, and countless mixtures that fizzled into nothing—today, we did it. We made the potion.

The day began like any other, except Liam seemed even more frustrated than usual. He stood over the cauldron, his face a mask of concentration, gesturing impatiently for me to hand him ingredients. His movements were sharp, almost mechanical, as if he were conducting a symphony of alchemical chaos.

I found myself relegated to the role of a mere assistant, tasked with fetching and delivering the various components. Despite my irritation at being demoted for the day, I couldn't help but find a certain amusement in the task. He wanted me to hand him things, then hand him things I would.

It became almost a game—moonflower extract, foxglove, powdered bloodroot, and, on a whim, a dash of salt from the table. Liam's razor-sharp focus never wavered as he carefully added each odd bit I tossed his way. I wasn't even attempting to follow the notes, just letting myself pick whatever I liked. We'd been at this for nine years, I can always bring a little whimsy. One of us needed to at least.

And then…the mixture hissed and turned a vibrant electric blue.

"Unexpected," Liam murmured, his brow furrowing deeply as he peered into the roiling liquid. "The next item?"

I blinked, as surprised as he was. Letting my instincts guide me, I reached for the moonstone essence and handed it over. He added it, drop by drop, and we watched as the liquid shifted—blue to violet, violet to a deep, velvety black.

"Now... the blood sample," he whispered, steadying his hand before letting a single drop of blood fall into the cauldron.

I didn't dare breathe. For a moment, nothing. My heart sank—again. But then... slowly, the mixture began to glow, softly at first, a pulse like a heartbeat deep in the liquid.

"Liam... look," I whispered, hardly able to contain myself. The liquid began to shimmer, tiny sparks flitting across the surface like stars in the midnight sky. "Do you see that?"

His eyes were wide, incredulous. "It's binding. It's truly binding..."

A laugh burst out of me, wild and relieved, and Liam's eyes lit up at the sound. "I can't believe it," I said, my joy bubbling over. "We actually did it."

And before I knew it, I was kissing him. No thought, no hesitation, just joy, sheer, uncontrollable joy. Right there, in the middle of our cluttered, magical mess of a room, with the cauldron bubbling beside us and the very air around us humming with energy, I kissed him.

For a heartbeat, he went still. Shocked, I suppose. But then, he kissed me back, his lips warm and urgent, as if something long held back had finally broken free. The world narrowed to just this: the feel of his hand on the back of my neck, his breath against mine, the taste of him. And in that split second, I could see a thousand tomorrows with him, an eternity with him. And with the potion, we could turn him—

But he pulled away. Just like that, his breath ragged, his forehead pressed to mine. "Emma, I—" His voice was hoarse, filled with something caught between fear and want.

I held my breath, waiting. He stared at me for what felt like forever, his gaze sweeping over me.

Then, abruptly, he stepped back. The space between us seemed to stretch and grow cold. "We must test the potion," he said, his voice quick and detached. "On a human."

I swallowed, pushing down the sting of disappointment and forcing a bright, cheerful tone into my voice. "Of course," I said, trying to mask the disappointment that clung to me. "We need to know it works. But Liam, we did it. We actually made it!"

He smiled, but it was a careful, guarded smile that didn't quite reach his eyes. "Yes, but that's only half the battle," he replied, already turning back to the cauldron. "We need a volunteer. Someone willing... or someone with nothing left to lose."

"Right," I agreed, stepping back, my heart still racing. "We'll write to the fae. They'll find someone."

But my lips still tingled, and my heart—oh, my treacherous heart—kept beating far too fast, as if it were still hoping for more.

Journal Entry of Liam Matthews

6th day of the Dispute Moon, 1705

I WROTE MYSELF THE letter today.

We have made the potion, the one we've been chasing for so long. We shared a kiss, one that was both tender and charged with the weight of everything unsaid between us. I felt a profound connection, a love that has grown silently and steadily over the years. But as our lips parted, I was faced with the undeniable truth of my own fear.

Emma looked at me with such hope in her eyes, and for a moment, I was tempted to ignore the looming dread that has clung to me since I realized my feelings.

I've faced many things in my life, but the prospect of enduring a lifetime of self-inflicted pain is something I can't reconcile. To see Emma, to feel the weight of our love, for that moment, and then see it slip away due to time, in all its forms and definitions—it's a future I dread more than any physical suffering.

I almost didn't write it—the letter that will ultimately, somehow, send Emma back through time. As if not writing it would somehow make the words within— that she leaves me—untrue.

Time is a loop. It must be. I always wrote the letter, and she always brought it back to me. I cannot risk my past self not knowing her in some half-witted attempt to keep her.

I need to ensure that the letter is safeguarded. I've reached out to one of my former mage mentors. They have agreed to hold it within their coven, to keep it secure until the moment is right, two hundred and four years from now. It's a promise of her safety, of preserving the timeline, even as it brings an end to our time together...

Emma's Diary Entry

16th day of the Dispute Moon, 1705

Dear Diary,

It's been odd, tiptoeing around each other. We've found the cure... and yet, my looming departure casts a pall over the achievement. This should be a time for celebration, a triumphant moment to savor, but instead, there's this distance between us. We kissed *again* today, and I'm sure it will only get more awkward.

Maybe I shouldn't kiss my long-term friends when we share a living space.

The end is certainly near though. The fae arrived this evening, just after sunset, bringing with them a test subject for our potion.

I heard them before I saw them: fae guards, their wings slicing through the air like blades. There's no mistaking their arrival; they don't sneak up on you. They descend like a storm, deliberate and unyielding. Even after ten years absent from them, I know the sound of a fae appearance instinctively. Prince Rian practically brought a parade whenever he appeared for diplomatic meetings with Demara.

I stood in the doorway, watching as three of them touched down, cloaked in shimmering hues of silver and blue. One cradled a human in their arms. He looked... well, he looked like death—skin stretched tight over bones, eyes sunken, with breath so shallow it was barely there. Another fae held Elder Fintan, who pushed away from his grip with a haughty air. I fought the urge to scowl at the sight of him.

Elder Fintan brushed off his elaborate blue robes and attempted to glare at us with the same icy superiority he had displayed during our first meeting, where he had voted for the extermination of my kind. "We had planned to bring a condemned criminal, offering him reprieve if he survived this test," he declared, his voice dripping with disdain. "But the High King, in his wisdom"—the way he said it made it sound like an insult—"suggested an alternative."

Which, of course, was why he is the High King, I thought with a trace of bitterness. Perhaps Fintan had forgotten, in his centuries of existence, that all vampires gain the gift—or curse—of immortality.

My gaze shifted to the boy held up by the fae guards. Young—too young. No more than twenty. His eyes darted around like a cornered animal, full of fear but not a word passed his lips. He just trembled.

"It's alright," I said gently, stepping closer. "This won't hurt... much. And if it works, you'll have an entirely new life."

A hollow laugh escaped his lips. "I'm already dying," he muttered. "What's a little more pain?"

Liam moved beside me, calm and composed as ever. "We'll begin immediately," he said, his voice even. "What is your name?"

"Wallace," he whispered, voice raspy like crumpled paper.

Liam offered him the vial. "Drink this. All of it."

Wallace hesitated, his eyes flicking from Liam to me, his hand trembling as he took the vial. He drank, grimacing. "Tastes like... metal."

"That's the binding agent," I said, forcing a light tone. "Now, stay still."

I watched as a hint of color crept back into his cheeks, but it wasn't enough. The actual test was still ahead. I stepped closer, feeling the familiar ache in my fangs. It had been so long since I'd tasted human blood, since I'd felt that electric rush. I leaned in, my lips brushing against his skin, and bit down. The taste hit me like a wave: rich, warm, intoxicating. I had forgotten how... good it was. How it made every part of me come alive. For a second, I wanted more, wanted to drink deeper—

But I pulled away, leaving Wallace gasping beneath me. "What... what now?" he asked, his voice trembling.

"Now, we wait," Liam replied, eyes fixed on mine, something unreadable in his gaze.

Elder Fintan huffed impatiently. "How long will this take? Girl," he snapped, "how quickly do you kill when you feed?"

"I don't," I growled back, the human blood still humming through my veins. Liam reached for my hand—a rare touch, if I forget the kiss from a few weeks ago—and it was enough to ground me.

The minutes stretched on, dragging into what felt like hours. Wallace's breathing grew shallow, his skin paler. Doubt flickered in Liam's eyes, mingling with the fear that we might have failed yet again.

Then, Wallace jerked, a violent shudder rippling through him. His eyes flew open, bloodshot but alert. He gasped, clutching his chest, and for a heartbeat, I thought we'd truly killed him. But then his breath steadied, his gaze sharpened, and he looked at me, intense and bewildered.

"I feel... strange," he whispered. "But not... dying."

A grin crept onto my face. "You're not dying. You're turning."

His skin seemed to glow with new vitality, his eyes flashing with the keen awareness of new life. He looked down at his hands, flexing them as if they belonged to someone else. "I'm... still alive?"

"As alive as we get," I replied, still smiling. "Welcome to the night."

Elder Fintan grunted, less impressed than I hoped. "I'll report this to the council. Expect a letter requesting your presence soon. Governor Harrington grows impatient."

After a quick lecture in 'here's how to be a vampire,' the fae took Wallace—still dazed and disoriented—and left as swiftly as they'd come. The room seemed emptier now, the air thicker with the unsaid words and unspoken emotions that had lingered between Liam and me. We weren't just tiptoeing around each other, it was an immersive dance.

Liam broke the silence, his voice steady but carrying an edge of resignation. "Nearly time," he said. "You'll certainly be on your way soon."

I met his gaze, trying to inject a note of hope into my voice. "But our friendship doesn't have to end just because I'm leaving." Almost flippantly, to hide how much I wanted it, I suggested, "I could turn you, find you in 200 years. Continue on, as we have been. Be something more."

His expression hardened immediately. "No."

"But why not? It worked! I could—"

"No, Emma," he cut me off, voice sharp. "Because you're leaving soon."

"Yes, but when?" I pressed. *Could I stay?*

He just looked away, his jaw clenched tight. "You don't get it," he said at last, voice low and tense. "You won't be here, that is immutable. And I'll be here. Alone. For two hundred years or more, waiting for you to come back—if you ever do. That's not giving me a choice. That's simply another demand. Another burden to bear."

His words cut deeper than I wanted to admit, both his sentiments and the continued confirmation that fate will force me back to the future. "And you think it's easy for me?" I shot back. "Knowing I have to go, not knowing when or if I'll ever see you again? You're my... my best friend, Liam. The person I want to see when I wake up in the morning and before I go to sleep. Yours is the voice I want to hear, no matter how biting it might be."

He shook his head, frustration flashing in his eyes. "It doesn't matter. You're returning. I can't just... wait centuries, hoping."

My chest tightened, anger and something else tangled together. "So what then, Liam? We just—what? Pretend none of this happened?"

He stepped closer, voice softer but still firm. "I'm saying... maybe we shouldn't start something we know will end too soon."

I hated how reasonable he sounded, but before I could argue, his mouth was on mine. This kiss wasn't like the last—it was deeper, hungrier, as if he was trying to say everything he refused to give word to. His hands cradled my face, mine tangled in his shirt, and for a moment, it was just him, just us.

But too soon, he pulled back, his forehead resting against mine, his breath hot and ragged.

"What was that for?" I whispered, my heart pounding.

"A good memory of me to take with you." he murmured. And then he kissed me again, softly.

"And that?"

"One for me to keep." And then he pulled away, clearing his throat, his expression carefully blank. "I'll prepare another batch of the potion if you'll check the supplies for the council's demonstration."

And here I am, scribbling it all down alone in my room, feeling foolish and... conflicted. After ten years here, after all the growing I'd done, you'd think I'd know what to do.

Note left by Emma for Liam

We're running low on salt. I'll run to town. Also, I've been trying a new technique for distilling the essence of foxglove. It would cut down on half the amount! I'll fill you in on the details tonight.

Emma's Diary Entry

29th day of the Dispute Moon, 1705

Dear Diary,

I should have known better. The warning voice in the back of my mind, insistent and nagging, had been telling me it was too risky, too dangerous to venture into town alone. And for what? Salt—the most mundane of our ingredients, something I'd added almost on a whim. Ten years of hiding, of only going anywhere with Liam, ten years of painstakingly crafting a potion to shift the tides away from hating vampires, and I'm undone by something as trivial as salt.

But I was stubborn, as always. I wanted to prove that I could handle it, that I didn't need Liam hovering over me like some overprotective guardian. That I was strong enough, worthy enough, to wait for.

Now, as I lie here in bed, every breath sending sharp waves of pain through my ribs, I can admit to you, Diary, that I was wrong.

It started innocently enough. The market was alive with bustling activity, full of noise and life. For a moment, I almost felt like my old self back in Fuil—like the girl who could walk through any crowd with confidence, who could laugh and chat with strangers without a care in the world. But that girl doesn't exist here, and I've been foolish to pretend otherwise.

We've been somewhat isolated from news of the violence. Certainly, we've sent the High King and his Council reports, and they've sent back requests that we try again. In the larger towns where we sourced the rarer ingredients, there were certainly quite incendiary news articles pasted on walls, but no violence to be seen. And we've never been re-called before the fae council, and no one ever brought up the idea to exterminate Aislean again. Perhaps I was in a bubble of protection. Perhaps Liam somehow shielded me from the worst of it.

Now, I wish he hadn't, but this is in no way his fault.

I don't know what gave me away. Perhaps it was the way I moved too quickly, too gracefully, or maybe it was just a spark of otherness that they caught in my eyes. Maybe the lump from years ago had been nursing a grudge against me and spread rumors about what I was. Someone shouted, "Vampire!" and that was all it took. The crowd turned on me in an instant, their fear twisting into something ugly, something violent.

I tried to get away, but there were too many. Hands grabbed at me, rocks and fists followed, and I went down. I felt the sharp crack of a rib breaking under a boot, the sting of a knife grazing my arm.

Somehow, I managed to drag myself away after they'd left me bleeding and battered in the dirt. I suppose I was lucky they didn't try to finish me off right there. "Let her suffer and bleed out," a voice snarled.

Lucky me, they still know so little about vampires, that only a wooden stake can actually kill us. But violence is still violence, and wounds made by a sliver of wood or not, it hurt.

I was too slow. By the time I made it halfway home, I could barely keep my eyes open, let alone stay on my feet. It was more likely that I'd trip and impale myself, completing the villagers' cruel intent. And that's when I saw him: Liam, storming down the path, his face a mask of raw worry and fury.

He didn't say a word, just scooped me up as if I weighed nothing. I remember trying to apologize, to tell him I was sorry for being so foolish, but the words wouldn't come. I must have passed out because the next thing I knew, I was here, in bed, Liam pacing the room like a caged animal.

He's furious, of course. Not at me, though I half-wish he were. No, he's angry at the world, at the townspeople, at himself for not being there to protect me. I tried to tell him that it wasn't his fault, that I'm not some delicate flower in need of constant guarding, but he wouldn't hear it. His hands were shaking as he bandaged my wounds, and when he finally spoke, his voice was rough, filled with a kind of desperation I've never heard from him before.

"Emma, you can't do this again. I can't—I won't lose you. Not like this."

There was something in his eyes—a raw, aching vulnerability—that made my heart skip a beat and my breath catch. But before I could respond, he turned away, muttering about fetching blood to help me heal, leaving me alone with my thoughts and the throbbing pain.

And now, as I lie here, replaying that moment over and over in my mind, I know what I should have said. I should have told him that I don't want to live a life where we're both just surviving, where he hides his feelings because he's afraid of what might happen next. Because I could have died today, he could die tomorrow, and my staying or leaving this time does nothing to change that.

I should have told him that I want more than this half-life we've built, more than a partnership of necessity and duty. I want him, and if we're both afraid, maybe that's exactly why we need to stop pretending and face it, together.

Journal Entry of Liam Matthews

29th day of the Dispute Moon, 1705

SHE—IT WAS—I CAN'T.

I've always believed she'd be leaving me to return to her time, not, not because she—

I will not even consider it.

Emma's Diary Entry

6th day of the Harvest Moon, 1705

Dear Diary,

I think I'm losing my mind. Or, more accurately, Liam is pushing me to the brink. He can't seem to keep his hands to himself, which would be a lovely development if it didn't also come with him pretending he didn't want to touch me at all. Every time I turn around, he's there, fingertips skimming across my arm like he's trying to memorize my skin. And the kissing—oh, the kissing. Yesterday, he kissed me three times before breakfast. The first was just a soft press of lips on my forehead while I was still half asleep to 'wake me up,' and the second, barely a brush of his mouth against mine when he brought me a cup of tea. But the third... the third was something else entirely. It was the kind of kiss that makes your knees weak and your head spin, the kind that steals your breath and leaves you wanting more, always more.

If he doesn't want this, he's doing a spectacularly awful job of showing it. And I can't decide what's worse: the weeks he spent avoiding me after the first kiss, or this maddening dance we're doing now.

At least the tiny shivers that come after every kiss take my mind off the bruises.

Emma's Diary Entry

10th Day of the Harvest Moon, 1705

Dear Diary, I couldn't handle it anymore. I finally had to say something this morning.

After breakfast, when he brushed his fingers over my arm again, almost unconsciously, I followed him to the makeshift library we've created downstairs. I perched on the edge of the table, where stacks of books swayed precariously. His gaze dipped to where my skirt had inched up, exposing more leg than usual, and I caught the way his fingers curled, like he was physically restraining himself from reaching out to touch my skin.

"You know," I said, keeping my voice light, "for someone who claims not to want me, you certainly have a hard time keeping your hands to yourself."

His brow furrowed as if he might argue, but then that infuriating half-smile appeared. "An astute observation," he said lowly, closing the space between us. The air felt thick, humming with the tension we always seem to carry between us.

"But nothing has changed," I reminded him, tilting my head to meet his gaze. "We still don't know when I'm leaving."

For a moment, he just looked at me, as though weighing some internal debate. Then, slowly, he reached out, tucking a loose strand of hair behind my ear. "Perhaps I've decided it's worth it," he murmured, his thumb tracing a soft line along my cheekbone, "to live like you're not leaving... until you do."

I blinked, taken aback. "So we're just going to pretend I'm not a ticking clock?"

"Yes," he replied simply. "Let's pretend."

My heart skipped a beat. "You mean it?"

He nodded, his eyes soft and warm in a way I've never seen before. "I mean it, Emma."

So, we agreed. We'll live like I'm not leaving, like I'm not a breath away from vanishing. And somehow, that simple decision feels freeing. He doesn't have to hold back, doesn't have to measure his words or guard his touch. I can kiss him when I want to, touch him when I need to, and imagine, just for a little while, that we have all the time in the world.

We haven't discussed it yet, but I think this means he'll let me turn him. He didn't want to wait for me before, when there was nothing, truly, to wait for. We made no promises to each other. But I can't stand the thought of him growing old without me, his hair silvering, his body weakening while I stay as I am. When I return to my time to visit an overgrown grave.

No, he understands now. And when the moment comes, he'll let me do it. He has to.

Emma's diary Entry

11th Day of the Harvest Moon, 1705

Dear Diary,

Time closed in.

We were testing the limits of our new arrangement earlier this evening, sitting together by the fire. I was in his lap, my arms wrapped tightly around his neck, and we were kissing like we'd been starved for it. The intensity of it, the hunger—I felt like I could drown in him, and he would gladly let me. His interest was obvious, pressed against the vee of my legs. A minute longer and I might have started begging.

But, of course, there was a knock at the door. A piece of parchment slid silently under the crack, and we broke apart, our breaths still mingling in the air between us. With a resigned sigh, I crossed the room to pick it up, the High King's seal glaring up at me in crimson wax.

Even after ten years in the past, I still despise correspondence.

"Time to face reality, it seems," I muttered, trying for a smile as I scanned the letter that would pull us back from this fragile, stolen moment of intimacy.

"When?" Liam asked, his voice rough, his lips still flushed.

"We need to leave tomorrow to make it in time," I replied, frowning. Only a day to bask in this... whatever this is.

Liam stood, a shadow cast long and dark as he came up beside me. His expression clouded when he noticed the second piece of paper—a hastily scrawled note warning of rogue vampires plotting to sabotage the council meeting and attack, to stop the potion from being shared.

A chill swept through me, a shiver of phantom pain from my fading bruises. "An attack?" I whispered, my eyes lifting to meet his.

His jaw clenched. "We've spent ten years on this. I'm not letting a few rebels ruin it now."

"I know," I said quietly. "But if they're planning an attack, we could be walking straight into a trap. It's not just us—everyone there will be at risk."

He met my eyes, his face etched with worry. "You don't have to go, you know. Let me handle it. Stay back."

"Between the two of us, I am the one who can't die without a stake," I pointed out dryly, although that will change soon enough, if the potion is approved by the fae.

"And yet, I'm the one with the warmage training," he countered, his tone matching mine.

"Then we'll just have to be careful," I said, firm.

He smiled, a small, wry smile, and lifted his hand to cup my cheek. "And I'll have your back," he promised.

I leaned into his touch, warmth spreading through me. "Together," I whispered, letting the word settle between us, like a vow.

We leave at dawn. And if there's one minor consolation to the interruption—beyond potentially saving my entire species—it's that Liam will have no excuse not to share a bed with me at the inns this time.

Journal Entry of Liam Matthews

13th Day of the Harvest Moon, 1705

THE JOURNEY BACK TO the portal was far less grueling than our initial trek. The landscape, though still dark and foreboding, seemed less hostile, perhaps because my spirit was lighter. It's remarkable how the prospect of a return to the familiar can shift one's perspective. I suppose it's much like how our feelings for each other have transformed the way we see the world.

Emma walked beside me, her hand occasionally brushing against mine—a touch that has become a source of comfort and strength. We spoke little, our words rendered unnecessary by the deep understanding we now share. The weight of our admissions from earlier hangs in the air between us, a bond woven from both our spoken and unspoken confessions.

Last night, we found ourselves in some ramshackle inn, walls thin enough you could hear a whisper through them. Only one bed in the room. Emma looked at it, then at me, with that challenging gleam in her eye, perhaps remembering our first trip. I half expected her to suggest I sleep on the floor just for the jest of it. But instead, she cocked her head to the side, letting her long blonde hair fall towards her waist.

"It's only sleep," she said quietly, an echo of our first night together at that first inn. "Will you be with me this time?"

I nodded, afraid my voice might betray me, that it would crack with everything I felt for her. We settled in bed, her body tucked against mine, my chin resting on the top of her head.

She's made me so maudlin, and emotional.

"I'd be with you forever if I could," I told her, my words barely more than a breath.

She pulled back, her gaze tripping over my face as a smile bloomed over hers, the sight that never fails to break something open in my chest. "My Liam," she said before kissing me.

We stayed like that, tangled together, her heartbeat steady against mine. I held her close, trying to memorize the shape of her against me, the way her hair smelled like the wind. I knew I shouldn't let myself hope, shouldn't imagine more than this moment... but how could I not? I've fought against this for so long, and now it's here, it's real, and I don't want it to slip away.

When the morning came, neither of us wanted to move. I could feel her breath warm on my neck, her fingers tracing small patterns against my chest. "Maybe we could just stay here," she murmured, half asleep, "forget about the council, the potion, everything else."

I smiled, knowing it was impossible but loving her for saying it, anyway. "If only it were that easy."

She looked up at me, her eyes more serious than I'd ever seen them. "It can be," she insisted. "Just for a little while longer."

I nodded, kissed her forehead. "Just a little while longer."

And we waited as long as we could. She's stepped out now for her morning ablutions as I write this. I'm reminded again of our last trip to the fae council, where I imagined all that could come, all that we were walking towards. Now, we're walking toward what might be the end of all this—whatever "this" is. Whatever happens at the council, I'll face it. But for now, I'll cherish the time we have left. I'll hold on to her with everything I have.

Emma's Diary Entry

14th Day of the Harvest Moon, 1705

Dear Diary,

I'm sitting here, in the cold, unwelcoming room of the council house, waiting for the inevitable. I'm trying to distract myself with the sounds outside—the clatter of carts, the murmur of voices, the steady drip of rain against the windowpane—but all I hear is the echo of our conversation from last night. All I feel is the sting of what he said.

We had arrived back in the city, found a room to stay in near the council house. It was late, and the city felt heavy, as if the weight of all its responsibilities pressed down on us. We were tired, but I felt... light, hopeful, even. We had slept so close these past nights, tangled together in ways that felt as if we'd finally untied all the knots between us.

That first night, he'd held me, his voice quiet and certain as he said, "I'd be with you forever if I could."

Forever. It's a word that's lived on the edge of my tongue for so long. I thought it meant he was finally ready, that he'd turn for me, be with me in a way that time itself couldn't steal from us. And why not? He's aging—I see it in the lines around his eyes, the gray threading through his hair. I told him so this morning, as we were getting dressed, trying to prepare ourselves for what the day would bring. I told him he didn't have to fear the end, not if he took the potion and let me bite him. "We could have eternity," I said, trying to sound light, playful. "You and me, forever."

He stopped then, stared at me with that deep, serious look of his, the one that always makes me feel like he's seeing right through to the core of me.

"Emma," he began, his voice already edged with that tone he uses when he's preparing to argue.

"Just hear me out," I insisted. "We could be together for as long as time exists. No limits, no end."

"No," he said softly, but firmly. "I'll take you for as long as I can have you. But I won't turn."

I felt my heart drop. "But why not?" I asked, my voice breaking. "You said you'd stay with me forever, Liam. That's what you said, just last night."

"I meant it," he replied. "My feelings are everlasting. But not like that. I can't... I can't do it, Emma."

"Can't or won't?" I snapped, anger rising like a wave inside me. "We've spent ten years together as friends, Liam. And who knows how long we'll have as lovers? You say you want to be with me, but then you refuse the only way we could actually have forever?"

He sighed, running a hand through his hair, looking so tired, so worn. "Emma... You know my feelings. But I can't live two hundred years waiting for you. That hasn't changed. I'll take whatever time we have left, but I can't do that to myself because we're scared of the end."

"So, you're telling me you'll watch yourself grow old, die, and leave me to find your name on a grave when I return?" I could feel my voice rising, my heart pounding against my ribs. "Why should I accept that, Liam?

He just shook his head. "No matter how long you stay, it will not be long enough," he murmured. "And I don't want to live forever knowing that."

I didn't know what to say. I felt like I was drowning in his words, in his refusal. "Then tell me," I demanded. "Tell me when I'm leaving. Tell me when the letter says I'll be sent back. If you know it's another ten years or fifty years from now... If you know we get that long together and you're still saying no, then fine, maybe I could accept it. Maybe. Because we'd at least have a life together."

But he just closed his eyes, shook his head again. "I can't, Emma. I can't tell you that. All I know is it won't be long enough."

Something inside me cracked. "So, what, then? You're just giving up on us before we've even started?"

He shook his head. "I'm not giving up. I'm holding on to what we have, what we can have... while we still have it."

I turned away, my hands clenched into fists. "Then you're asking me to let go, too," I said, my voice thick with emotion. "To accept that this is all we get, that you've already decided how much time I'm worth."

"That's not what I'm saying," he protested, reaching out to touch my arm, but I pulled away.

"It feels like it," I said, unable to keep the tears from welling in my eyes. "It feels like you're choosing to end this, to make me leave before I even have to."

"Emma, please," he murmured, but I couldn't stand to hear it, couldn't stand to feel like I was the one holding on when he was already letting go.

I stormed out then, needing air, needing space, needing something that wasn't him and his endless reluctance to let himself be truly mine.

Liam. Stubborn, infuriating Liam. I should have known he'd resist this. He's the most cantankerous man I've ever met, like an old wolf that growls before he shows his belly. I had to worm my way into his life—no, I practically kicked the door down. At first, he tried to push me away, tried to hide behind that prickly exterior. But I got past that, didn't I? I chipped away at his walls with every argument, every sarcastic remark, every shared glance over a steaming cup of tea. I made him see that he didn't have to be alone.

But now... now I think he's built a new wall, a stronger one. One made of fear.

I should have known he'd do this, that he'd find some way to protect himself from what he thinks is inevitable. That's what this is, isn't it? Not some grand, principled stand against becoming a vampire, but him trying to shield his heart from what he's decided is going to happen. Decided that I'll leave, and he'll be the one left behind.

I thought I'd broken through that fear. I thought, after ten years, I'd made him see that he doesn't have to face everything alone, that he doesn't have to keep me at arm's length to survive. We were a partnership, a team. We were everything to each other for ten years.

But it turns out... maybe I was wrong. Maybe he's still protecting himself, clinging to some idea that if he doesn't change, if he doesn't turn, then it won't hurt as much when I leave.

All he's doing is building another wall. And I'm left standing outside, wondering if I can keep waiting for him to open the door.

Excerpt from Annabelle Harrington's personal accounting of the 1705 events

14th day of the Harvest Moon, 1705

...While waiting for discussions to begin, I found myself lingering near the side of the great hearth, its flames creating long shadows upon the marble floor. My husband's voice, strong and resolute, intermingled with those of the fae councilors. How powerful he is! It was then, amidst the indistinct murmur of negotiations, that I noticed a most unusual exchange between two figures.

There stood a woman of uncommon beauty, her skin a warm, golden hue that seemed almost to shimmer in the dim light. Her blonde hair fell in loose waves about her shoulders, and her eyes held a fierce light that reminded me of a predator on the hunt. But she did not seem menacing—no, there was a kind of grace about her, a strength that went deeper than her appearance. Beside her was a man, pale and pasty, with a drawn look about his face, as if he had weathered many sleepless nights. His brow was furrowed with worry, his hands clenched tightly at his sides. He wasn't handsome. But striking, most certainly, and his features were softened by something more, something tender.

They seemed to be in the middle of an argument, though their voices were kept low, as if they feared being overheard. The man reached out, grasping the woman's arm with a touch that was both firm and pleading. His pale face was flushed with some deep emotion. She pulled back slightly, her golden skin catching the light in a way that made her seem almost aglow. Her expression was tight, defiant, her lips pressed into a thin line. There was fear there, and something like yearning. It reminded me of my early years with Ali, when we were courting and Mama believed Ali not worthy of me. How wrong she was.

The couple *was* quarreling, that much was clear. The man's voice grew more urgent, though his words were still tempered with concern. I saw her eyes soften then, her anger ebbing like the tide. She reached out to touch his face, a fleeting caress that seemed to hold a world of meaning. His own hand covered hers, and for a moment, it seemed as though they were the only two souls in that crowded chamber. Whatever had passed between them, it was more than mere words—it was love, powerful and unyielding, forged in fire.

Then, as if aware of being watched, they separated, their expressions turning guarded once more. It was then I saw it—a flash of fang as she moved, her lips parting ever so slightly. My breath caught in my throat. A vampire, and yet... she did not seem a monster, but a woman with a heart that beat as fiercely as my own. And he, a human, holding her hand as if he feared to ever let it go. I marveled at the sight.

How strange, I thought, that in such a place, amidst all this talk of war and peace, I should find a glimmer of something else—a hope, perhaps, that even in the darkest of times, love might yet find a way to bridge our differences. If a vampire and a human could look upon one another with such tenderness, such unwavering devotion, then surely there was hope for the rest of us...

The fae council called the meeting to...

14TH DAY OF HARVEST MOONFALL   105TH YEAR OF BEARACH

THE GAZETTE

HISTORIC COUNCIL MEETING SHAKEN BY ROGUE VAMPIRE ATTACK

COUNCIL CHAMBER, CUMHACHT-What began as a historic day of hope and reconciliation was violently interrupted when rogue vampires launched an attack on the Fae Council Meeting yesterday evening, leaving devastation in their wake and taking two hostages, including a high-ranking vampire diplomat.

Representatives from the human and vampire contingents appeared to review the long-awaited 'Turning Potion,' a creation said to hold the potential to transform the nature of the mortal/immortal long-standing conflicts. The demonstration, witnessed by Council members, human emissaries, and vampire leaders alike, showed the potion's effectiveness on a human volunteer, seemingly offering a path toward peace that many in our realm have long thought impossible. The atmosphere in the council chamber was tense but cautiously optimistic as the potion's creators—vampire Emily [information unknown] and a mage ally—stepped forward. Elder Muireann who presided over the proceedings, lauded the potion as a potential "new dawn" for our relations with the vampire covens, while expressing concerns over its practical application and the political ramifications for the fae.

CONTINUED ON PAGE 2

THE GAZETTE   14TH DAY OF HARVEST MOONFALL, 105TH YEAR OF BEARACH

CONTINUED FROM PAGE 1, VAMPIRE ATTACK

Duchess Lidia, representative of Fuil, and Governor Harrington of the Human Territories of Latha joined the Council's discussion, debating the logistics of imposing this solution on the rogue covens that have, for decades, refused to align with any formal governance. The proposition sparked heated discussions, with Elder Fintan and Duke Varian arguing that bringing these rogue covens to heel would require significant force—potentially escalating into open conflict.

Yet before a resolution could be reached, the council chambers were plunged into chaos. A group of those rogue vampires, who must have been hiding within the crowd, launched a sudden and brutal assault.

Witnesses report seeing shadows erupt from the far corners of the room as spells of darkness were cast to blind the fae guards, followed by a barrage of arrows and smoke bombs. Several fae were injured in the initial onslaught, and panic ensued.

HOSTAGES TAKEN AMIDST THE MAYHEM

In the midst of the turmoil, the attackers seized two high-profile hostages: Duchess Lidia herself and the female vampire believed to be one of the creators of the Turning Potion. While the vampire was unnamed, sources within the Council identified her as 'Emily,' a key figure in the recent diplomatic efforts. Their fates are currently unknown, and it is feared that the rogues may use them as leverage to demand concessions or derail the Council's efforts to establish a treaty.

CONTINUED ON PAGE 3

THE GAZETTE — 14TH DAY OF HARVEST MOONFALL, 105TH YEAR OF BEARACH

CONTINUED FROM PAGE 3, HOSTAGES

Eyewitnesses describe the rogue vampires as organized, coordinated, and armed with enchanted weaponry. They vanished as quickly as they appeared, taking advantage of the pandemonium to escape with their captives. High King Bearach condemned the attack, calling it "an act of cowardice and a desperate attempt to halt the progress of peace."

In the wake of the violence, the fae council has called for an emergency session to address the escalating threat posed by rogue vampire factions and to consider military responses. Governor Harrington and other human emissaries were rushed to safety, but there are concerns that this attack could further destabilize already fragile negotiations.

The fate of Duchess Lidia and Emily remains uncertain, and the Council urges caution. "We are dealing with adversaries who have nothing left to lose," said High King Bearach. "Their brazenness today shows they are willing to go to any lengths to prevent a resolution."

The incident has cast a shadow over what was meant to be a turning point in our history. Yet, for now, the future remains uncertain, the outcome hinging on the fate of the hostages and the resolve of the Council to face the challenges ahead.

ANYONE WITH INFORMATION ON THE ROGUE VAMPIRES OR THEIR WHEREABOUTS, CONTACT CHIEF GUARD CEALLACH IMMEDIATELY.

Emma's Diary Entry

14th or 15th Day of the Harvest Moon, 1705

Dear Diary,

Somehow, I ended up in this vampire stronghold, one of the lesser used ones, I suspect, given the taste of mildew in the air and the echo of dripping water somewhere far off. They didn't bind me after their interrogation, which I suppose is a mercy, and failed to check my pockets.

Which is why I'm able to write in you now, Diary. If only I'd had a hidden blade or at least a useful charm, but no such luck. They must think I'm harmless. Or maybe they did notice the diary when they threw me over their shoulder and stole me from the meeting. Maybe they enjoy the idea of me writing my last thoughts before they slit my throat.

How very considerate of them.

It began at the fae council meeting. Liam and I had reconciled enough to present, though the argument about his future as a vampire is still at issue. He cannot forgive me for pushing him toward immortality, and I cannot forgive him for not wanting it. There's too much life in him to squander on death. But we shelved our quarrel long enough to stand before that sea of fae and vampire eyes, and I held my chin up like the princess I once was.

We had another human volunteer, another young boy with earnest eyes and shaking hands. Sweet Wallace brought him in, the volunteer clinging to him. But even with his fear, he took the potion with surprising courage. I bit him, and as we knew it would, he turned right there, shivering and sweating, falling into Wallace's arms like a newborn fawn struggling to stand. Right there, in front of them all, he became one of us. The room buzzed with disbelief. Some gasped; others whispered. But there was no denying it.

And then came the debate. Duchess Lidia and Governor Harrington, eyes gleaming with the thrill of possibility, were ready to take up their positions. What did it mean, they asked, to have a potion that could turn humans into vampires at will? What would it take to bring the rogue covens to heel? Treaties, they said. Force, they said. And just as they began to plot, the rogues struck.

An explosion, a burst of chaos that shattered the calm we had cobbled together. I barely had time to grab Liam's hand before the room descended into madness—shouts, screams, bodies colliding in a blur of violence. I lost sight of him quickly; he's trained for this sort of thing, and I am not. I stumbled through the smoke and confusion, trying to find a way out or at least a corner where I might not be trampled.

And then they snatched me. Their way of saying congratulations, I suppose. They dragged me out of the council chambers, across the moor, and into the carriage like a sack of potatoes. Not the most dignified of exits, but I wasn't exactly in a position to argue.

When they finally deposited me in this gloomy little stronghold, I tried to talk sense into them, but that was like trying to reason with a brick wall—one that hisses and bares its fangs.

"You don't need to do this," I told them earlier, leaning back in the chair they so graciously tied me to. "It strengthens us to have more join our ranks," I said, trying to appeal to their greed. "Think of the numbers, the power. More vampires means more strength."

One of them—a particularly tall and surly fellow with a face that looks like it's been chiseled from old wood—snorted. "We kill you, girl, the potion dies with you," he growled. "We're not fools."

"Oh, you're not?" I replied, Liam's snark clearly infecting me after our years together. "Because you're acting like a bunch of them. You think my death is going to stop this? You think I'm the only one who knows how to make it? Please. You're more backward than I thought."

I barely had time to finish my sentence before I felt the sting of his hand across my face. Hard enough to split my lip, but not enough to do much more.

"Watch your tongue," he snapped. "We could make this much worse for you."

"And yet you haven't," I pointed out, spitting blood onto the cold stone floor. "What's the matter? Afraid we're related? That I'm your long lost... niece?"

And truly, Diary, I wonder! Mother and Father won't be born for another fifty years at least, but what if one of these idiots is a hapless uncle? It would be just my luck, wouldn't it? Descended from a bunch of murderous fools.

He didn't answer. Just glared at me, then turned and left. The others followed, leaving me alone in this damp, stinking room with nothing but my thoughts and this diary. I've no idea what's happened to the Duchess. For all I know, they've spirited her away somewhere else, or perhaps she's already met her end. I can't recall her history well enough to know for sure. If she's alive, hopefully she's somewhere less miserable than this, and if she's dead, well... there are worse things.

My heart twists at the thought, but I force it down. No use worrying over what I cannot know.

I'm afraid, Diary, no matter I'm trying to remain brave. My history in this timeline is unknown. Time is a loop, I'm sure, but the loop can end without my returning. I've done what I was brought back to do: create the potion with Liam.

And Liam—his future is assured, at least for now. He hasn't written himself the letter—the one that sends me back to him—and he must stay alive long enough to do that. He'll get out of this. Maybe he'll join the fae in trying to rescue us. They may not know exactly who I am, even the High King doesn't know who I was in the future, only that I'm a time traveler, but they wouldn't leave a Duchess here.

Would Liam still come for me, though, if the High King deems us mere casualties in this conflict? I believe so. No matter our last argument, he wants as much time with me as he can have.

Any amount of time will not be long enough, he'd said only this morning. Assuming it is still the day of the fae meeting and I wasn't unconscious for long.

But—

Diary, is it possible that Liam has never told me when I'm leaving because... because I die here?

Emma's Diary Entry

6th day of the Flower Moon, 1909

Emma's Diary Entry

8th day of the Flower Moon, 1909

Dear Diary,
   I-

Emma's Diary Entry

10th day of the Flower Moon, 1909

Dear Diary,
 I'm home but—

Emma's Diary Entry

11th day of the Flower Moon, 1909

Dear Diary,

I don't know how to begin. My hands are shaking so badly I can hardly hold the pen, let alone find the words. I feel as though I'm still covered in Liam's blood—his scent, his warmth... all of it is fading so fast. There's this awful emptiness in my chest, like something vital has been torn from me, and I don't think I'll ever stop feeling it.

But I have to write it. I have to put it somewhere, or I'll lose myself in the darkness.

I'd waited days in that cell, the rogue vampires coming once a night to throw containers of blood at me and make various threats. The walls seemed to close in on me as I huddled in a corner, my heart pounding like a drum. It was agony, the waiting. And then things changed.

It happened so quickly, all of it. One moment, I was alone in that damp, miserable stronghold, my head spinning with thoughts of who might come, or if anyone would at all, if I'd die in that cell, 200 years in the past. And then suddenly, the door burst open with a crash that shook the walls, and there he was—Liam, standing in the doorway, eyes blazing with fury and determination. And he wasn't alone; a group of fae warriors stood behind him, their magic flaring like distant stars. For a second, I couldn't breathe.

The look on his face when he saw me, Diary... I will carry it with me always. Relief, anger, determination, all mixed together. I threw myself into his arms, and he held me so tightly I thought I might break. "I've got you," he kept whispering against my ear, "I've got you." And for a moment, just one fleeting moment, nothing else mattered.

But there was no time. As soon as we left the cell block, the battle crashed around us like a storm. Rogue vampires lunged at us with bared fangs, their eyes feral with hunger, and fae magic crackled in the air, tearing through them like lightning. I was terrified, my heart in my throat, but there wasn't any time to think—not when death was so close, not when every second counted.

Liam pushed me behind him, withdrawing a sword from his scabbard with his other hand. But he didn't use it, only to keep any incoming enemies at a distance. And he didn't need it, his free hand striking out with magic I'd known he'd possessed but never seen. Power crackled in the surrounding air, a furious, beautiful display of all he was capable of. I knew he was trained a battlemage, but I'd never seen him fight like that. It was breathtaking and terrifying, a force of destruction and protection all at once. If anyone could get us out of there, it was him.

We moved through the stronghold like that, Liam clearing a path with magic, me at his side, desperately trying to stay close. I kept glancing over at him, marveling at the strength, the sheer determination in every movement. He was risking everything for me, and all I could think was how much I wanted to make it worth it—how much I wanted to live, to see him safe.

And then... it happened. I heard him gasp, a sharp intake of breath, and I turned just in time to see an arrow piercing his side. He staggered, his face blanching, and my heart stopped. I leapt in front of him, grabbed his sword, and swung at the nearest vampire with a scream that tore from my throat, fury and fear blurring my vision.

Somehow, we pushed our way outside. The night air hit us like a cold slap in the face as we emerged from the fortress, the sky above a tapestry of inky black punctuated by pinpricks of starlight. The sounds of violence still roared around us and I realized the stronghold hadn't been in the Aboveground, but in Avalaruin, just outside one of those spindly forests found in the fae world. *How will I get him home?* I thought, nearly delirious with fear.

Liam collapsed into my arms, and his blood soaked through my clothes, hot and terrifyingly sticky. "No, no, no," I whispered, pressing my hands against the wound, desperate to keep him with me, to stop the bleeding. But blood seeped through my fingers, no matter what I did. "We need a healer. Liam, stay with me. Please, stay with me."

He was pale, so pale, more than usual, more like death. But he smiled up at me, his eyes so soft. "It's okay," he whispered. "It's going to be okay, Emma. Everything will work out... how it's supposed to."

"Stop being so stubborn," I nearly screamed. "You're losing too much blood. We need the healer's help."

My gaze darted around the battlefield, searching for anyone who could heal the deep gash across Liam's abdomen. That's when I saw her, the woman in white—a fae healer, running toward us through the smoke and blood. I almost sobbed with relief, but just as she was about to reach us, an injured fae warrior stumbled into her path, collapsing at her feet with a gut-wrenching cry of pain. The healer's expression morphed into one of concern as she knelt down beside the fallen fae, her hands hovering over his wounds.

"No!" I howled, but Liam's hand squeezed mine, his grip so weak it was barely there.

"Don't worry," he murmured, his voice so calm.

"You're going to be fine," I insisted, my voice frantic, desperate. "You have to be. You haven't written the damned letter!" The words came out almost hysterically, my mind racing. "You can't die, Liam. You haven't written the letter yet!"

But then... he looked at me with such sadness, such calm. "No... I already wrote the letter."

The world seemed to tilt. He had already written the letter. Which meant he'd already done his part in this cursed time loop. It meant... it meant he could.... And now...

[Ink splotches as pen remains pressed hard against the paper]

He was in my arms. He was... blood was...

"Liam, no," I remember choking out, my voice breaking. "No, you can't—don't you see? If you've written the letter, then—then you could... please, let me turn you. We can figure it out, I'll wait, I'll wait 200 years, I'll stay here, whatever it takes, just... Please, don't leave me. Not here. Not like this."

His face was so peaceful, and it made my heart feel like it was shattering. He reached up, his fingers brushing my cheek, leaving a smear of blood behind. "Emma," he said softly, "you need to conserve your strength to get out of this place, back to the farmhouse. And everything will be fine."

"Stop saying that!" I snapped, the fear and frustration bubbling over. "How can you be so certain? You're bleeding out!"

"Don't worry about me," he breathed, his voice thick with emotion. "Get out of here."

Tears spilled over, hot and desperate. "We can make it, Liam, we have to make it. Please, please... don't leave me."

His thumb brushed away my tears, his eyes soft and full of something I couldn't bear to see. "I love you," he whispered, so faint I had to lean in to hear him. And then...

And then... it happened.

The pull. That terrible, wrenching feeling as time itself reached out and tore me away. I screamed, fought against it with everything in me, but it was useless. His hand slipped from mine, his face fading into the mist as everything around me blurred.

And then...I was back here, the original letter—one I thought Liam destroyed—clutched in my hand. I landed in the throne room, covered in blood and dirt, interrupting Demara's meeting with her guards about me.

It... it had only been a few hours, in this time. I'd been pulled from lunch with Cerdan in the afternoon and by evening, I was back. In Fuil, in my once home.

But I wasn't truly back, was I? Not really. Because the person who left... she isn't the one who returned. She never will be.

Emma's Diary Entry

15th day of the Flower Moon, 1909

Dear Diary,

The healer says I need to keep writing. I'm not sleeping—the bed like ice, the sheets too heavy—so I might as well do something.

Demara and Clara found me in the morning, still dressed in yesterday's clothes, staring out the window into nothingness. I didn't turn when I heard the door open. I felt their eyes on me, the weight of their worry pressing into my back. I didn't care. I couldn't care.

Demara was the first to speak. Her voice, usually so steady and commanding, wavered. "Emma... have you slept at all?"

I didn't answer. I kept my gaze fixed on the gray, fogged glass, half-expecting—half-hoping—to see some sign of him, even though I knew it was impossible.

Clara was sweet, gentler than she'd been when I was a child, which only confirms what I already know: I'm different now, a different Emma returned to them.

She tried to rouse me with correspondence and playful threats of meetings, bringing up the Turned leader again. But I didn't even respond. There was no teasing response from me. Those idle worries are just that.

"Emma," Clara tried again, more softly, stepping closer. "There must be something to be done. Please... talk to us."

Finally, I turned to face them. "Talk about what?" My voice was raw, barely a whisper. "There's nothing left to say."

They exchanged a look. I could see the pain on their faces, their helplessness, their confusion at how to help me. It almost made me laugh—a bitter, hollow sound that never quite reached my lips. They'd never understand. No one would.

"We spoke with the Oracle again," Demara said, trying to sound reassuring. "But she... she had nothing more to offer. She said that what has happened is as it was meant to be."

"As it was meant to be?" I snapped, turning fully toward them now, anger rising like bile in my throat. "Is that supposed to comfort me? That this—this loss, this emptiness—is all part of some grand plan?"

Clara flinched, but Demara held her ground, though I could see her hands tremble slightly. "We also spoke with the mage," Demara continued, her tone softening. "The one who gave you the hallucinogen... she said something about traveling, but—"

"Nothing," I interrupted. "She had nothing. None of them do."

Demara nodded reluctantly. "Yes, none of them had any more answers."

A silence fell over us, heavy and suffocating. I could feel Clara's gaze, her concern like a physical touch, but I couldn't meet her eyes. I was too raw, too exposed. Too broken.

After a long moment, Demara spoke again. "Perhaps a visit to the farmhouse would do you some good."

I'd given her an edited version of my trip, and the farmhouse—and its host—were the star.

I knew what she meant. She thought it might bring me closure, or peace, or some other meaningless comfort. But I didn't need closure—I needed answers. I needed to know if there was anything left of the place where I became... this person.

Clara pursed her lips hard. "We discussed this," she whispered to Demara as if I couldn't hear.

I ignored her. "Yes," I said, surprising them both. "I want to go there. I need to."

Clara immediately looked concerned. "Emma, it could be painful—"

"I don't care," I cut her off sharply. "I need to see it. No matter what it looks like now."

Clara opened her mouth to protest, but Demara silenced her with a look. "If that's what you want, Emma," she said gently, "we will find it."

It isn't what I want, Diary. But the farmhouse is all that I have left of my time in the past. And of him.

Emma's Diary Entry

20th day of the Flower Moon, 1909

Dear Diary,

It took several days. Days of endless searching with the historian, poring over old maps and documents. Every hour that passed felt like a lifetime. I kept you, Diary, with me, clutched tightly in my hands, refusing to let anyone else see it. It was the only thing I had left, the only connection to that time, to him. I used it to help piece together where

I had been, but I kept most of the details to myself, guarding them like precious jewels in a world of thieves.

Finally, we found it. A forgotten place, buried deep in the records. A small, remote farmhouse that hadn't existed in any official documents for over a century. When we arrived, the sky was overcast, a dull gray that seemed to suck the color out of the world.

The farmhouse was gone. Burned to the ground. Only charred remnants remained—blackened beams and crumbling stone walls, half-buried in overgrown grass. The sharp scent of smoke lingered, as if the fire had only recently died, even though I knew it had been years.

I stood there, staring at the ruins, numb. There was no sign of life, no trace of what had happened there. Just ashes and silence. The place where he'd lived, where we'd loved, was nothing more than a grave now, unmarked and forgotten.

"Emma..." Clara's voice was hesitant, careful, as if afraid to touch me with it. "We should return. There's nothing here."

I didn't move. I couldn't. "No," I said, my voice no more than a whisper. "Not yet."

Clara exchanged a worried glance with Demara, but they didn't push me. They stood there, waiting, giving me time. But time was meaningless now. It stretched on forever, a bleak and empty road with no end in sight. I knelt on the ground, brushing my fingers over the charred remains, hoping, praying for something—a sign, a clue, anything.

There was nothing. Just ashes and dust and silence.

Clara knelt beside me, her hand on my arm. "Emma, please. You're hurting yourself. Let's go."

I pulled away from her touch, my hands clenched into fists. "He's gone," I whispered, the words tearing out of me like a wound being ripped open again. "He's gone, and there's nothing I can do to bring him back."

Clara's face crumpled, and she looked away, blinking back tears. "I know," she said softly. "But you still have a life to live, Emma. You must keep going."

I laughed then, a harsh, brittle sound. "Keep going? For what? For who?"

"For yourself," Clara said, her voice steady. "And for him. He wouldn't want you to... to give up like this."

I stared at her, my eyes burning. "You don't understand," I hissed. "I don't have anything left."

We stood in silence for a long time, the wind whispering through the ruins like a ghost. Eventually, Demara spoke. "Maybe... maybe you should try to get back to some kind of routine," she suggested hesitantly. "Meet with the leader of the Turned, perhaps. It might help. To see someone who's been helped by what you did."

I turned to her, my face twisted with grief. "And Liam," I said, my voice hard and sharp. "What he did. Make sure his name is remembered too." No longer should we believe a mage lost to time created the potion. Liam did.

Demara nodded. "Of course. His name won't be forgotten. I'll make sure of it." She ran her hand over my hair, petting me like Mother used to. "You did a wonderful thing, Emma. Even though it hurts now, you changed the world for us. You did that."

Clara agreed. "That battle you mentioned, it was the beginning of the end. Only a handful of years and the Lord came to power himself. Let yourself be proud of what you both did." She clapped her hands, as though the decision had been made. "Best to get back to normal, with your experiences to better guide you."

"Set up the meetings, please," I told her, a strange sort of calm settling over me. Not peace—no, never peace—but a resignation. A numb acceptance of the endless days ahead.

"My sister," Demara said, voice light, "becoming so responsible. Who would have thought?"

Not me, Diary. Not Liam, likely, either. But time changes us all.

I used to believe I could dodge fate, outwit it with charm and sheer stubbornness. But fate is patient. It waits, lurking around every corner, until you have no choice but to face it. I'm ready now. Ready to face mine.

As Clara dropped me off at my room, she prattled on about my upcoming schedule, further suggesting that I find some way to move forward rather than continue to wallow like I have over these past two weeks. "You have an endless life to live, Emma," she reminded me softly. "And you're not alone. We're all here for you."

I nodded, though I wasn't sure if I believed her. How could anyone be there for me when the one person I needed was gone?

But life must go on, they say. And I have a very long life to live.

Excerpt of letter from Lysandra, Cerdan, and Alina

YOU ABSOLUTE MENACE,

You've always been impossible, but this is a new level of infuriating. You disappear from Rye Lantern—*vanish,* no less—without so much as a cryptic farewell, and now, after weeks of silence, we hear you've been taking meetings with dignitaries? Emma, *dignitaries?* Something you'd have sooner faced a stake to avoid not long ago. Have you finally taken leave of your senses?

We wrote you a letter for Fate's sake—*correspondence*! That alone should show you how concerned we are...

Unopened card from the Turned leader attached to a bouquet

Sent after their meeting was first canceled

To the Lady Emma,

I have heard of your recent ordeal, and I wish to extend my sincerest hopes for your swift recovery.

Tales of your bravery and resilience are well known in my domain, but I imagine that even someone as formidable as you is entitled to moments of rest and respite.

There is much that I would discuss with you when you are feeling yourself again. Matters of mutual importance. But for now, I merely wish you well and hope that the days ahead bring you strength, clarity, and perhaps even a measure of peace.

Until we are able to meet, I will remain ready to assist you in whatever way I can. Our paths will cross soon, I am certain of it.

Yours in patience and anticipation,

—L.W.M.

Clara's Daily Accounts

**29th day of the Flower Moon, 1909
To be placed in official Aislean records**

She sat with her back to the door, her posture stiff but resolute. She had forgone her usual frippery, donning only the simplest gown from her wardrobe. The Emma I helped raise would never have settled for such simplicity; anyone with eyes could see how she had changed from her trek to the past. I've clung to the hope that the girl I knew remained within her, buried beneath the surface of this grieving woman.

The Turned Lord arrived, his attire as formal as ever. In another world, he and Emma might have found common ground, no matter how staid he is. That quiet resolve within him might have balanced well with her bright boldness.

Emma certainly never sussed out why I was so adamant they meet. He likely had, one can only propose a one-on-one meeting with an eligible lady, princess or otherwise, before suspicions arise. But he never revealed his thoughts to me. It was only in the slight tension of his hands, the twitch of his brows, when I continued to turn him away that told me how much he desired to meet her. And even now, each day, he has returned, ostensibly to complete the 'meeting' scheduled on that fateful day—of Emma's departure and return.

There was a vast chasm between them on this day. Though they were always opposites, I had seen no genuine issue there. And despite his nearly two centuries of being a vampire, he had been turned before he was fifty—a significant age difference, certainly, but not insurmountable. Especially now, with Emma having lived ten years in a single day. But her heart remained broken.

Lord Matthews hadn't greeted her yet, merely watching her back with an intensity that suggests he was waiting for my cue. Clearing my throat, I slipped between them.

"Princess Emma," I began, "allow me to *finally* introduce our esteemed ally, Lord Matthews, leader of the Turned."

She sighed, as though greeting him took more energy than she was willing to use.

"I promised you forever," he rumbled in that deep voice of his, gravelly and resonant in the cavernous room.

Her head jerked up as if yanked by an invisible string. She turned, eyes wide and glistening with tears. His own eyes betrayed a hint of moisture, and I sensed that there was something more to this moment than I could understand.

"Anything else is not long enough," he finished.

In an instant, she leapt from her chair and threw herself into his arms, her sadness melted away. She was more like my Emma, the tempestuous and happy-go-lucky child I saw grow up. Lord Matthews caught her and dipped down to her lips, kissing her with such passion I felt I was surely intruding.

Quickly, I left the room, letting the door close softly behind me. Though somewhat perplexed, I had a nagging feeling that I was missing a crucial piece of the puzzle. But then again, that's Emma for you.

Brushing my hands against my gown, I searched for Demara. Her own love life remains unfulfilled, whereas Emma's future seems to hold no such concerns...

Epilogue

Dear Diary,

I can't even describe what I felt seeing him there. It was as though my heart restarted. It feels fantastical to even write these words, as if my pen cannot capture the enormity of this moment.

Once we'd fallen into each other (and likely embarrassed Clara enough to leave), I cataloged the differences between my Liam and Lord Matthews. He looked like the man I left behind, perhaps a little more silver threaded in his black hair, a few more lines at his eyes—though they looked like laugh lines, which lightened my heart.

Time had shaped him into someone powerful, commanding even. He held me on the floor of the grand hall, his arms stronger than I remembered, his frame sturdier. But there was still gentleness in the way his hand pressed against my back, harkening to those moments when he showed me his softer side.

The story of how he became this man—this leader—came out in fits and bursts. "After I realized what an idiot I was being," he said, "I did whatever I could to make sure I'd come back to you."

He spoke of the battle I thought had claimed him. A healer found him after I'd left him lying in his own blood and despair, patching up his wounds. The fae gave him a commendation for his work in finding the stronghold. As I thought, he worked tirelessly for days to find it—me.

"It was Duke Varian who Turned me," he continued, his voice growing quieter still. "Lidia survived. Barely." He paused, his dark eyes glittering with the weight of memory. "Her brother's death—your dear relative—set the throne in motion for your grandfather. And Varian, ever the strategist, saw my usefulness."

My throat ached, but I managed a whisper. "He convinced you?"

"I refused it for years." His lips thinned as he gazed past me. "Expecting to return to my farmhouse and my solitude. But life... life had other ideas." A faint smiled bloomed over his expression. "Varian and Lidia ensured I was occupied, endlessly meddling with their potion and their emissaries. Even the Harringtons became allies."

"Is that why you agreed?"

His eyes snapped to mine, unguarded. "No," he said bluntly. "What changed was this: I realized the utter futility of clinging to solitude. I had a life I could live, a purpose I could carve out. Why stubbornly waste decades unhappy when a few centuries would bring me happiness?"

So he accepted, letting Varian take from him, and becoming something more than mortal. What he hadn't expected, of course, was the political ramifications that came with it.

"Little did I know," he said with a smirk, "that becoming a Duke's progeny would make me royal-adjacent in the eyes of the Aislean and fae. I became the de facto leader of this new species."

I couldn't help but laugh, the absurdity of it breaking through the heaviness. "Poor Wallace," I teased lightly. "If they'd realized I was a princess, perhaps Wallace would have had his day, and you'd have been free to go on your merry way."

The hours slipped away as he continued his tale: how he helped broker alliances and brought order to the Turned, how he built a life. When he finally fell silent, we simply looked at each other.

And then he leaned in. His lips met mine, the kiss deliberate, controlled, but filled with an intensity that left me breathless. His hand slid into my hair, his fingers tangling gently but firmly, anchoring me to him. It was as though every unspoken promise, every unvoiced longing, had been poured into that single moment.

When we broke apart, his forehead rested against mine, his breath warm against my lips. "Two hundred and four years since we last did that," he murmured, his voice as smooth and precise as ever, though softened by the ghost of a smile.

I laughed, though it came out shaky. "Worth the wait?"

He tilted his head slightly, his dark eyes meeting mine. "Worth eternity," he said, his voice a silken promise.

And now we lay in my bedroom, Liam asleep beside me as I finish this entry. I glance over at him, his face soft in the lamplight, so different from the sharp, commanding presence he carries while awake. His hand rests near mine on the blanket, close enough that I can feel the warmth of his skin.

There is still much to be done, Diary. Demara has her suitors to choose from, and I remain her heir. The weight of my lineage still looms, though tonight it feels easier. Liam is a sovereign himself now, his place among the Turned as unshakable as mine in the Aislean court.

Clara will be back soon, no doubt, with a barrage of lectures and expectations. My friends deserve answers. The *court* will demand answers. The Turned will demand leadership.

But for now, there is only us.

Liam's letter to himself

To Myself,

I know you'll think this is a trick when you read it, some elaborate ruse crafted by the fae or an enemy with too much time on their hands. But I assure you, this letter is from me. From us. And yes, it's as maddening as it sounds.

By now, you've met her—the time traveler. She spent a day with you as a child, mere minutes when you're barely a man grown. And when she reappears in your thirtieth summer? Not long enough.

She is going to upend your life. She will irritate you beyond measure with her impulsiveness, her way of waltzing through life as though it exists for her pleasure, and her uncanny ability to dismantle your carefully laid plans. You will call her reckless, insufferable. And you will be right.

But you will also be wrong.

There will come a moment—perhaps while she's laughing at your expense, or arguing with you about something trivial—when you'll realize she has become the center of your world. And that's when you'll understand why I wrote this letter.

She must leave. And someday, you will not begrudge a second of your time together.

The time you have with her is fleeting, but it is yours. Treasure it, even when it hurts. Especially when it hurts. Because no matter how much you wish you could change the outcome, you cannot. Her path is set, as is yours. You'll need these memories when you spend the rest of your life alone. Do not take them from us.

Until then, be kind to her, even when she tests your patience. Be honest, even when it feels like a risk. And above all, don't waste the time you've been given. It will not be long enough.

She is worth every moment.

—Liam

Further reading

IF YOU'RE INTERESTED IN more of my writing, check out my website (**kmalady.com**). You can find information about my other projects, like *The Ascend Trials* (a romantic YA portal fantasy all about subverting tropes), *Threads of Fate* (an NA romantic fantasy series adapted from greek myths), and more!

And if you're looking to spend more time in the trope-ics, check out the below:

<u>SHE WHO BINDS THE FAE PRINCE</u>
A spicy romantasy novella

<u>SHE WHO FREES THE SELKIE</u>
A sweet adventure romantasy novella

<u>SHE WHO CLAIMS THE ALPHA</u>
A (sweet & spicy) interactive romantasy novella

<u>AND MORE!</u>

ABOVE-GROUND LUNAR CALENDAR

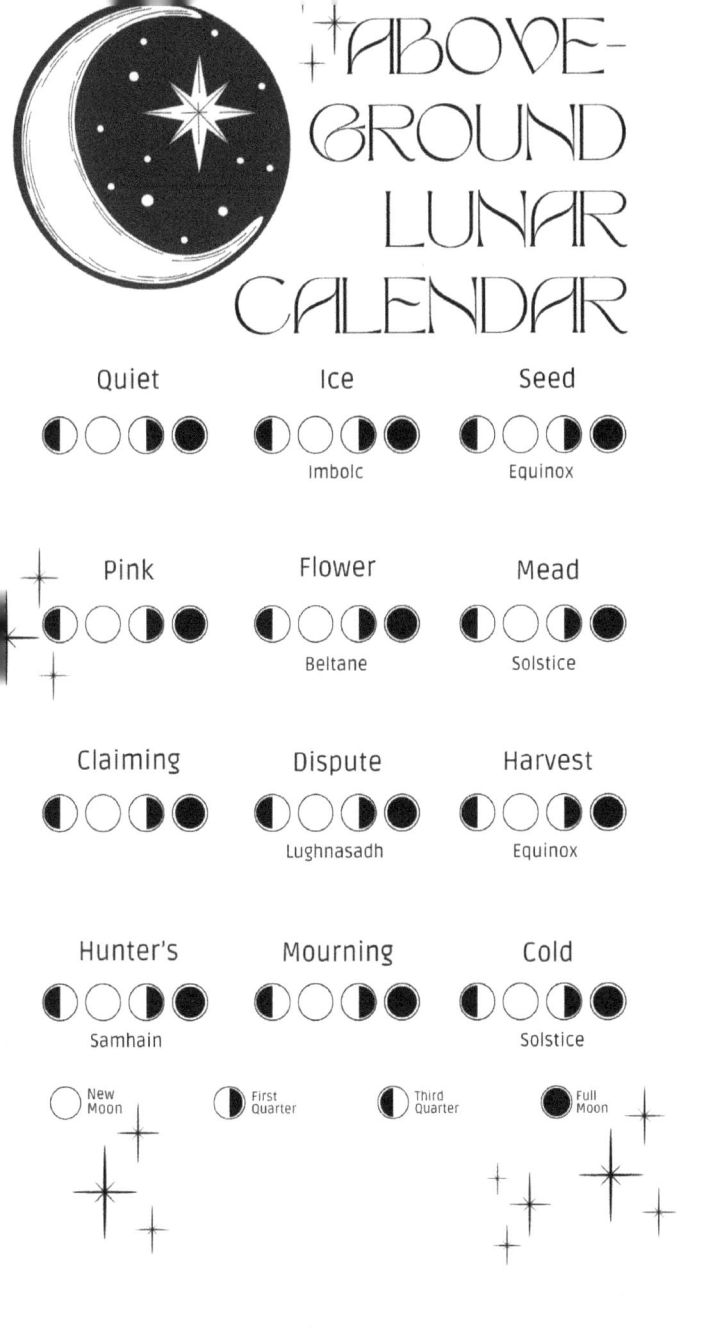

Quiet
Ice
Imbolc
Seed
Equinox

Pink
Flower
Beltane
Mead
Solstice

Claiming
Dispute
Lughnasadh
Harvest
Equinox

Hunter's
Samhain
Mourning
Cold
Solstice

○ New Moon ◐ First Quarter ◑ Third Quarter ● Full Moon

www.ingramcontent.com/pod-product-compliance
Ingram Content Group UK Ltd.
Pitfield, Milton Keynes, MK11 3LW, UK
UKHW032024070225
454812UK00004B/257